PRISCILLE'S
ALIEN
PIRATE

DEDICATION

This is for my readers who had to find their own path in life.

BOOK - MA

This book is intended for mature audiences for adult language, sexual content, and violence. It deals with themes of religious trauma, domestic abuse, abduction, possible drowning, and other adult topics.

VÒLLⱯ IAN GLOSSARY

NŎKHÚ – A SHIP'S SECOND IN COMMAND (SIMILAR TO A UNION REPRESENTATIVE, OR A FOREMAN)

CHÙSĤŮ – THE WEAPONS EXPERTS ON A SHIP

PEHOLOE – ELDERS WHO HAVE LOST THEIR GHA

VÒLLØ – ONE OF THE MAJOR ALIEN RACES ON SHOJO, USED IN THE SAME WAY WE USE HUMAN.

SHÈPERŒŞA – WOMEN BLESSED BY THE BASO SHEVA TO EXPLORE SHOJO'S MYSTERIES

ĜHE – A SPECIAL TYPE OF WOOD FOUND IN THE VALKARRAN MOUNTAINS

JISA – A ANATOMICAL SHIELD THAT PROTECTS THE SKIN. THE VÒLLØ HAVE IT NATURALLY, SOULMATES DEVELOP IT THROUGH THEIR BOND.

ĜHA – PERSON WHO MAKES MY SECOND HEART BEAT, SOULMATE.

GINGI LEAF – A NATURAL PLANT USED AS AN INGESTIBLE DRUG. WHEN GINGI IS USED SEPARATELY IT MEANS ADDICT.

ĠEĜÌĈHŒ – A BOVINE-ESQUE CREATURE THAT IS GENERALLY FOUND IN PRAIRIE-TYPE AREAS

LLIGE – LIKE RICE

D'O GO CHU MERCHU – MY ENERGY IS YOURS

ŘÙŞAU'Ù – A TRADITIONAL BONDING CEREMONY ON SHOJO

J È – YES

Ĕ ĻIQĚ ĜU VA Ĭ LU – YOU SHOULD NOT BE HERE

HØ – A DIMINUTIVE FOR CHILD

RIŞA – DANGER

B'IVA – A GAME PLAYED AMONG SAILING SHIPS ON SHOJO

NEKED'I – A GAME PLAYED WITH CARVED CHIPS

PRONUNCIATION GUIDE

MEKHO - MAXE-SO

PRISCILLE - PRIS-ILL

SERKHA - SERX-HA

KOVILU - CO-VEE-LU

WUPESO- WOO-PAY-SO

VALKARRA - VAL-CAR-UH

YISO - YEE-SO

VÒLLØ - VAH-LOW

ĜHA - SAID LIKE A PLEASING SIGH 'AHH'

ĜHAJO - AHD-JAY

ŘŮṢAD'Ù - RRR-SAW-DO

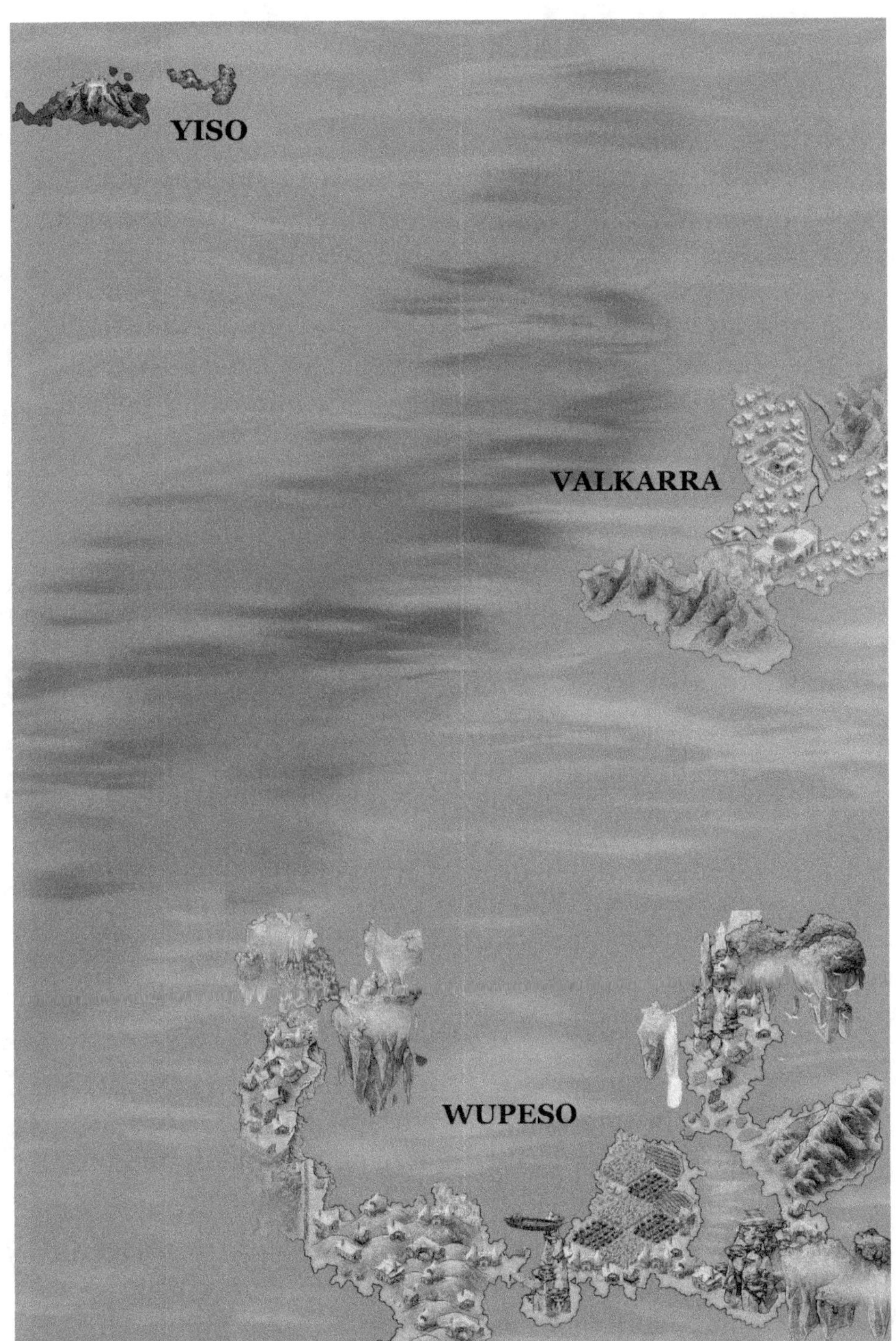

YISO
VALKARRA
WUPESO

Chapter One

Mekho

The Valkarran's ship was rarely ever worth raiding, but this sun cycle, it held a treasure far beyond any I had ever seen. With the Death of Baso Sheva, this treasure should not have existed. So many died, even of my own crew, from thousands of different tragedies. Stories of freak storms, mass illness, and divine intervention circulated the world I knew. And all this death made it nearly impossible to find a young woman at all. Let alone one such as *her*.

My Jewel was shorter than the Valkarrans rushing about their ship with a voluptuous frame. She had warm hair the color of the dune lands, braided neatly down both shoulders. It framed her pale, round face. From what I could see, her body curved like the waves. I wanted those waves to crush against me like I was her land.

Snapping my looking glass closed, I feel a burn as my second heart begins to beat inside my chest. The beautiful creature across the way is my *ĝha*.

Disbelief and happiness were like my twin-beating hearts in my chest. With every pump of one came more of the other. Pulling away my shirt, I smirked at the marks branding me.

We needed to cross the Rough Waters. Now.

"Ready the cannons crew. We have a ship to loot," I call, finding my place at the stern. Kovilu, my *no ˇkhú,* is quick to respond, ordering Ngheza and Jajo aloft to rig the sails and the *chùŝhǔ* below to man the cannons.

My crew was much smaller than before the Death of Baso Sheva, but I remained blessed to be among eight incredible sailors. They were women I could count on in even the worst of storms. Their status as elders gave them the wisdom to deal with a wild captain like me, and I appreciated their advice, even when I did not want to hear it.

"You truly wish to cross the Rough Waters?" Kovilu asks, her mossy gaze swinging across the dark stretch of sea. "For the Valkarrans?"

Luckily, the deep sea was calm today. But even so, the Rough Waters wouldn't be simple to navigate. Because of the conflicting currents and the shifting of the land beneath the sea, maelstroms and gyres could pop up at the slightest disturbances. There were many tales about the Rough Water's hungry waves, created to warn sailors against crossing the section of sea for any reason. Greed being the worst offense. But I did not care. My $ĝha$ was with the Valkarrans, and Vova would guide my way.

"We must. My treasure is among them."

The Rough Waters would throw my ship back and forth, attempting to drag us to the deep blue beneath, but one way or another, I would reach the Valkarran ship on the other side. It held a treasure worth the trouble we had been through in the previous seasons. It contained a prize my crew would happily fight for. So, we would sail, and I would find the beautiful female on board, and I would make her mine.

Chapter Two
Priscille

I loved the ocean. Okay, well, I loved *this* ocean. On Earth, I never got to see the sea, regardless of being so close to it. The abbey was about a mile from the cliffs, but the point of my time there was to visit the abbey and volunteer. My mother didn't think it was a good idea to fall in love with the surrounding area when I would be cloistered away when I became a nun. Later, when I left the coast, I glimpsed the blue waters. But, glimpse aside, the closest I'd ever been the view was from the plane on my trip from The Coast to Las Vegas.

On this planet, I found my naivete both negative and positive. On Earth, I barely glimpsed the ocean. Sad. It meant I had nothing to compare this spacious blue view to here. Happy.

"I feel at home," Serkha admits beside me. I nod in agreement.

Though my soul was in rocky waters, and I did not know if God had abandoned me, the crisp sea breeze was doing wonders for my feelings of belonging. For a moment, it almost felt as if my grief for Earth would one day be forgotten. It almost felt like the scars inside my soul were closing.

Leaning against the bow rail as the waves rush up to meet the ship, I feel blessed. It is my favorite spot on the entire vessel because here, I could watch the point of the bow carve through the bobbing peaks below. Though I had no direction spiritually, I had one physically, and seeing it fed my faith. My chosen view made me sicker than ever on the first day, but I didn't give up on it. After ten Shojo days, I could watch our path for hours without repercussions. I could feel grounded, knowing that I was finally heading somewhere.

"Can you see Baso Sheva inside the waves?" Serkha asks, following the line of the water to the horizon. According to Serkha, the Baso Sheva existed in every piece of Shojo. The sea was like the maiden, Vova, fresh and emotional. On our first night, she told me if I looked closely, I would see Vova at work, guiding us to where we needed to be. Since then, I took extra care to search the waves and my heart, but I couldn't see her, or God, in the tiny swells and crashing sprays. Even today.

"I'm sorry, I can't," I whispered, tearing my gaze away from the mesmerizing patterns. Disappointment was a dragging weight in my chest, and as it sunk inside me, I felt like I was dragging Serkha down with me. I didn't feel worthy of her interest in helping me. I didn't feel worthy of these adventurous experiences at all.

Still, Serkha smiled a gentle smile that made my heart clench. She did not feel dragged down by me, even though I felt like the worst shipmate, because she never asked me to help with the various chores, always sending me back to enjoy the air when I tried. She told me my only job on this journey was healing. For that, I could thank God. Even if he would not answer because I had plenty of healing to do.

Unfortunately, something about landing on this planet had left me incapable of seeing the work of the divine in each moment. And that feeling of disconnect slowly rotted inside me. I could feel the old, helpless Priscille crying for me to come back to her, but rock bottom is a hard place to be. So, I would continue to work on finding connection and meeting this unsung need inside me. My circumstances needed to change before my soul died completely, and I would go through any journey to make that happen.

Serkha brushed back a strand of my hair like my mother used to, tilting her horns to the right.

Serkha was comforting from the moment I met her on the path in Valkarra. She was Roxie's mother-in-law, and she had the strength to be. Yet, she was also soft and easy to talk to. She could direct her crew efficiently or stand here with me and assure me divinity was absolute, and I would feel it again. That I was worthy of feeling it again.

"You are okay, Priscille. All you are feeling is not without reason."

I nod, feeling the tears burn behind my eyes. Maybe the Vova was there because I cried a lot since we left. It had only been ten Shojo days, but I already missed Clara and the other human women. I missed the *peholoe* loft, and I missed the temple in Valkarra. Serkha was great, but as the captain, she was busy. There would be hours at a time when her work inundated her, and I was utterly alone. I didn't blame her, but it was easy to overthink without a gaggle of women buzzing around me with their own various issues. I hated feeling so alone.

A salty tear escaped, and I brushed it away angrily, huffing a deep breath. Through watery eyes, I met Serkha's gaze.

"I'm okay. I will be fine."

She nodded; her eyes narrowed on me like she was trying to confirm my words. Then, her eyes widened, and her jaw clenched. The energy seemed to shift in the air, and the hairs on the back of my neck stood on end. Her firm hands gripped my shoulders, and she was pulling me in close. Disoriented, half-pulled off my feet, her hands met my face, my arms wrapped around her. I thought she meant to hug me, but she pushed my arms down to my sides and hunched down to my level.

"Priscille, I need you to listen closely."

Fear spiked through me, drying my tears as I attempted to glance behind to see what Serkha had. Her fingers tightened slightly, keeping my attention, and a familiar dread crept into me. Whatever Serkha saw, it was enough to scare her, and her fear frightened me.

"Go to my quarters, lock the door. Don't come out until I come get you. I am the only one with a key, so don't open the door for anyone. Do you understand?"

With my cheeks squished beneath her hands, I nod, muttering my agreement. If we were in trouble, I wanted to help, but that simply wasn't my strength. I would only distract them, and I knew that. So, instead, I would do whatever Serkha told me to and stay out of the way.

"I'm going to let you go, and you're going to run straight for my cabin. Lock the door. Don't come out."

"Yes, ma'am."

Her fingers fell from my face straight to the hook at her belt. I was off like a shot, sprinting across the long deck and trying to understand what I was hiding from. The ladies of Serkha's crew were all geared up, and then a loud crash sounded, and the ship threw me sideways.

My body collided with the main mast, and I grit my teeth against the pain as I stood. *What is happening?* Still discombobulated from my time in the air, I searched for the door to Serkha's cabin, unable to ignore the chaos any longer.

Ropes with grappling hooks were thrown over the railing, tying us to another ship full of Vòllø people. Vòllø *pirates.* They were tugging their ship in closer, laying out a plank for them to cross over. I was frozen in place as I watched them work. Just like Serkha's crew, they moved in sync. They were a team, and everyone on it knew exactly what to do.

My body refused to listen to me as I ordered myself to get up. My eyes darted from one pirate to another, and then they locked on one standing beside the mast. He was the only male aboard the entire ship, and he was *smiling* as his crew prepared to board.

Fear was a stuttered cadence in my chest. I forced myself to my feet, stumbling to Serkha's door as my head throbbed. At another glance, I saw the pirates finally come aboard ours, and I doubled down on my speed. *Serkha's cabin – I need to make it to Serkha's cabin.*

The steady wooden door is feet away when I hear the clash of weapons. Someone screams, but I refuse to look. Swinging the door open, I slam it behind me and twist the metal lock closed. I give myself two seconds to react to the sound of battle before I find more ways to protect myself and pray.

Serkha's cabin is small but neat, aside from the few pages and utensils thrown in our rough stop. A solid wooden chair sits behind her desk, and her single bunk is cleanly made. As I search the room, I can't find a weapon, but I move the chair from behind her desk as an extra precaution. I slide it against the door, feeling safer after adding a barrier of protection.

Finding a place on her bunk, I curl in on myself, facing the door. I drag her pillow to my chest and try to make myself as small as possible as shouts and fisticuffs persist outside. I take a centering breath. Then, I send up a prayer. God might not be listening to me anymore, he might not have jurisdiction on this planet, but I pray anyway.

"Please, Lord. Keep Serkha and her crew safe. Please help us face this adversity. Your will be done." I whisper over and over.

"Your will be done."

Chapter Three
Mekho

The Valkarrans were not expecting us nor watching the edge of the Rough Waters. Truthfully, they never did. We would be upon them before they were ready, and it would give us the edge we needed. *Thank Vova herself.*

As my crew prepared to take their ship, I ordered, "Keep them alive. We are looking for a woman – hair like the dune lands, different than the Vòllø, shorter. Understand?"

The mere memory of her face through the looking glass was enough to bolster me.

"Yes, Captain." The crew responded only moments before we breached the Valkarran vessel. We didn't usually do much of this kind of piracy, preferring to sack ships in port cities along the mainland route or sink other pirates who acted as our competition. We found sailors in our line of work knew very little about things of value, while the people buying cargo knew it all. This meant we had a slight disadvantage, but with my *ĝha* aboard that ship, nothing could stop me.

Plus, my crew needed a little excitement in their lives.

The Valkarran vessel had been moving rather quick, but as our hooks dug in, the ship jerked sideways. Valkarrans went tumbling, sending one near the farthest rail over and into the drink. The ease of the latch satisfied me, but then I watched as my treasure sprawled across the deck. Her tiny head smacks against the mast, and I fist my hand at my side.

"Gentle. Sheva strike you. Gentle." I shouted, watching my crew adjust. My eyes were drawn to the unique female, even as our ships collided. She seemed frozen in place as we prepared to board, but when her eyes landed on me, she ran for the captain's quarters and locked herself in.

"Engage the crew. I get the captain." I call, stomping from my place beside the mast. It was bad manners to enter a captain's quarters without permission, after all.

"Yes, Captain." My crew responds.

Kovilu dropped a plank across the railing of our two ships, and I was the first to march my way across it. The churning sea was angry beneath me, rocking both vessels and challenging my balance, but I paid no mind. Life at sea made me well-equipped for jostling and gyrating. I focused on putting one foot in front of the other, using my tail to keep balance.

My feet were on the Valkarran's deck in moments, and my crew was right behind. A smaller woman immediately came after me with a sword, slicing at my chest with vigor but sloppy footwork. Stepping out of the way, I shot her a cheeky grin. I hear the boots of my crew members hit the deck.

"Meet Jajo; she would love to separate you from your sword," I explain, walking further onto the deck.

The Valkarrans ship was a nice vessel, and if I weren't emotionally attached to my own, I would consider stealing it. But unfortunately, my ship doubled as my childhood home – it was the last remaining piece of my mother. Their *ĝhe* wood railing, though? I could make a good trade out of that, even if it wasn't whole. That kind of wood was rare near the mainland.

As another one of the Valkarrans attacked me, I stepped aside, searching the crew for the sapphire woman who sent my treasure running. She is not afraid, standing back from her crew, awaiting my approach as she swings a tiny rope with a weapon attached to its end. It's sharp, but it will be ineffectual.

I hear a scream behind me and grit my teeth, trying to keep my swaggering air about me as I approach. I did not need to harm the Valkarrans. They simply held something of value to me. I only came to claim her, my treasure beyond no other. But, if they harmed my crew, I could not guarantee everyone would leave unscathed. And I really wanted to make that guarantee.

"You are not welcome here, pirate." The woman says, giving herself a little more rope to fight with. She was obviously skilled, though maybe a little rusty. The Valkarran women used to be much more adventurous but with the Death of Baso Sheva...

"I believe you have something of mine," I reply easily, dodging as her tiny, dagger-ended rope as it flies toward my face.

"There is no treasure here, only standard trade goods and *shèperœṣa*." She says, swinging again.

"Ah, yes. And one who is not *shèperœṣa*, right?"

Her eyes narrowed in my direction as I dodged another flurry of attacks. As we fight, I can't help but think there is something familiar about this woman, like maybe I had seen her before. Yet, that could not be possible. I hadn't crossed the Rough Waters since I was a boy; I had not seen the Valkarrans since I was a boy.

I approached slowly, forcing her to use less and less rope until she grasped the sharp piece of metal in her palm. My crew was behind me, doing an amazing job as many of this woman's crew lost consciousness or ceased fighting at the threat of a blade. Niti was already rounding them up and binding them to the mast.

"I don't know what you speak of." The captain lies, her eyes darting to her cabin.

"You seem like a valiant captain," I grin, my eyes flashing as her tiny weapon is driven toward my primary heart. My hand snaps out, crushing the bones of her wrist as she strains against me. She is incredibly strong, I admit, but the power of the Baso Sheva is on my side today. I tighten my grip slightly, giving a small twist. The weapon drops from her hand, clattering to the ship's deck.

Little does this woman know her attack would have been ineffective. The blade was simply too small. Both my hearts beat now. The closer I get to my prize, the stronger my *jisa*. Even so, I was a smart sailor. Leaving one's hearts unprotected was an easy way to ensure they stopped beating. So, as you can understand, I had to divest her of her weapons.

Catching the rope as it falls, I slip the tiny weapon into my free hand. Twisting one arm behind the captain's back, I hold the small blade to her side.

Together, we scan the deck so she can see the loss she and her crew face.

The deck is nearly silent now, and I breathe in our victory. My crew has successfully subdued the *shèperœṣa* of Valkarra, and those still conscious struggle against their captors, looking to their captain for guidance. There is no more clashing of weapons and shouting. Only quiet grunts of struggle and shuffling boots against the deck. My eyes fall back to the striking blue woman before me.

"I have no qualms with you, Valkarran. I simply want my treasure."

"Sheva strike you, beast," the woman spits, baring her fangs in a final stand against me. It brings a smile to my face.

This captain could not know of the tragedy my crew has faced, the loss I've experienced, the troubles I've faced as of late. She could not know the lengths I would go to for this one boon in my life. So, instead of monologuing and waxing poetic, I simply say, "She already has."

Chapter Four
Priscille

Dread fills my stomach at the silence on deck. Nothing about the atmosphere gives me reason to believe I'm in trouble, per se. The boat rocks back and forth gently. Sun streams into the cabin through the slatted windows at the back. The waves lap against the wood. The sound should soothe me, but it feels ominous. I stare at the door, and I know any minute, someone is going to try and bang it down. Someone is going to forcibly enter and drag me away. I can feel it. I can practically hear Abbess Carlow whispering, *"This world is not of God, it's of the Devil. Evils abound."*

I curl further in on myself, hugging my thighs for comfort. Footsteps approach outside. A casual, confident cadence.

"Your will be done. Your will be done." I whisper against the pillow, hoping they don't know I'm in here. The pirates. There are *real* pirates here.

The doorknob wiggles and a pitiful squeak escapes me until I realize the lock is turning. *Only Serkha has a key.* There is a solid *shunk* before the device disengages, and Serkha tries to open the door. Relief cools the adrenaline in my veins, and I spring from my spot on her bunk to move the chair. My legs still feel a bit like jelly, but my relief keeps me standing. Dragging the chair back behind the desk, I toss the pillow back toward the bunk and try to straighten my skirt.

Thank you, God. Thank you, Baso Sheva. Thank you, whoever saved me. I pray, fussing with my appearance so I don't look as if I nearly peed myself with fear.

The next time the captain tries to open the door, it glides open easily. The sun reflects off the sea, bathing the Vòllø in shadows, and I squint my eyes against the light. I'm too relieved to think – to notice this Vòllø is slightly wider than Serkha, that the horns curve in a distinct pattern. As only a silhouette, I don't notice a difference. Shooting forward, I wrap my arms around her.

Not her. Not Serkha. *Abort. Abort. Abort.* I scramble to release my arms, to pull away, but –

Strong arms come around me, and I panic. I let my legs go limp, expecting my captor to drop me, but he doesn't. Instead, his arms band around me tighter, pinning me against him. I struggle, but he speaks, and I find myself frozen in place.

"Calm, my *ĝha*. You are safe now, Treasure."

His voice must be magic because it feels like it settles into me like a healing salve. It makes me whole. Until this moment, I believed only peanut butter chocolate candies could do that. A man with a voice like peanut butter chocolate candies – my first miracle.

I allow myself to relax against him, tentatively bringing my arms around his waist again. My fingers twist in the soft linen of the shirt at his back, and my knuckles rest against well-developed muscles. As I press my chest against him, I feel the ridges of his abs against me too. Whoever this guy is, he's stacked. Strong.

Capable of crushing you in a single heartbeat. The voice is Abbess Carlow's, but I ignore her dramatics.

The man's hand comes to my head, smoothing down my frizzy braids, and I hear the happy sigh I make as if I'm no longer in my body. Being in his arms is like an out-of-body experience.

Maybe you're not in your body. Maybe this is God. Who else would have a voice like peanut butter candy?

Now that my eyes have adjusted to the bright light and shadows, I peek up at the man's face. My mouth drops open because he is stunning. Yes, the human women in Valkarra always teased me because I thought they were all pretty, but this man was a cut above the rest. He's not God, for certain, but he looks like the type to be worshipped. On the altar of a king-sized bed anyway. My mouth goes dry.

I hear Abbess Carlow's reprimand, *"Do not blaspheme."*

He has a sharp aquiline nose and a pleasing jawline. His skin is like a palette of bright, electric indigo, and his eyes are a stunning shade of gray. It's like if you carved a Hollywood hunk out of a chunk of lapis lazuli and cobalt. Or maybe you dyed him to match your favorite pair of jeans. This man's arms around me felt as comfortable as my favorite pair of jeans, that was for sure.

"Captain, we should go before they wake." Someone calls from beyond the door, yanking away my man's intoxicating attention. The interruption to whatever bubble we entered could have come faster as I'm reminded immediately this man is a pirate. He is here to steal something.

I renew my fight and try to pull out of his arms, but they simply flex against me, bulging into the soft portions of my body and molding us together further. It's like I made every crevasse to be held against this man, and my wiggling seems futile.

"Yes, one moment. Relax." He calls to them, returning his attention to me not a moment too soon. "Where are your things, My Jewel?"

If he thinks I'll tell him where the cargo is, he's mistaken. I struggle against him again, but he doesn't let up. I growl, "I'm not telling you where anything is."

His brows crinkle, and he glances down at his chest. Using one hand to tug his shirt away, he confirms his mate marks are there. Sparkly and teal, they seem to sing with light. Wait.

Mate marks.

He called me his ĝha.

Oh, no.

Chapter Five

Mekho

My markings are there, glowing with pride as I hold my *ĝha* against me. Still, she wiggles. And I cannot understand her words. Was she not with a crew of Vòllø? Does she not know the Valkarran language?

"Get your things," I repeat, "Let's get your things."

"Noh wey, yu pie-rat. Fhor-getit." She says, shaking her head vehemently and still struggling against me. I let her go, but without my support, she tumbles backward – as I expected. I am quick to respond, sliding my hand around her dainty wrist and tugging her forward. She gains her balance easily and rips her hand from mine, narrowing her tiny round eyes in my direction. Redness infects her cheeks, and she huffs a breath.

Is she okay? Is my *ĝha* sick? I can't help myself. My hand comes to her face, my thumb brushing across her velvety soft skin. It feels like the sacred flowers that grow along the coast of Vúzha island. Then, the color fades, and I realize it must be a normal human reaction.

"Stah-puh." She screeches, twisting her face away from my grip. Does she not want me to touch her? She is my *ĝha,* chosen by my goddess herself, delivered to me on the sea I love – and she doesn't want me to touch her?

I drop my hand to my side, ignoring the sting of my marks from her rejection. Before the Death of Baso Sheva, when you found your *ĝha,* it was like a celebration. Friends and family would cheer. The moment you showed the other your marks, you would tumble into bed together. But Baso Sheva died on Shojo for a time. I had to accept the situation may be different.

My *chùŝhŭ* arrive at the door behind me. They peek past my shoulders, and I stiffen. I don't like them looking upon her like this. She is frightened and angry. That much I can feel through our bond. But I trust my crew with my life. I should trust them with hers as well.

"Is this the treasure, Captain?" Lakhu asks, giving my *ĝha* a cursory glance. It's a respectful but curious look, and I keep still to allow them their curiosity.

"Yes. Loot any of the trade goods you find interesting. And find her belongings. I am going to get her to the ship." I respond.

"Yes, Captain." She responds, directing Ushu and the other sailors beyond the cabin. I would be surprised if they came back with anything. This had been their livelihood for so long that it was a long shot that the Valkarran's trade goods would be of any interest to them.

When I return my attention to my *ĝha,* she has taken a seat in the chair behind the desk. She sits with her arms crossed and her eyes narrowed in displeasure. It brings a smirk to my face.

"Aym naht goh-eeng whith yu." She says, in her odd language. She looks comfortable in her chair, and I wonder if she is struggling to understand me like I am her. I close my eyes for a moment to try and make the mental connection, but when my mind reaches out for hers, it reverberates like I smacked a stone wall.

When I open my eyes once again, her brows draw downward, and her lips pinch together. She doesn't move from her chair. I may not have been able to speak with her mentally, but I felt her stubbornness course through me. Whatever stand she tried to take, she dedicated herself to it.

"My treasure," I start, taking a step closer to her. Before I can say another word, she shakes her head sharply at me, then tilts it to the left like a disagreement. *So, she does know some* Vòllø *customs.*

"Noh. Mie naym iz naht trezh-urr. Mie naym iz Pris-sill," She pauses, glaring in my direction before angrily repeating, "Pris-sill."

"Pris-sill," I repeat, feeling the lightness and pleasure of it on my tongue, causing a ripple across my *jisa.* It must be her name.

"Priscille." She tells me, blending the sounds more smoothly.

"Priscille."

With a sharp nod, she seems to pause before tilting her head to the right. I've finally done something right, and I know my lovely treasure's name. And a beautiful name it is. Exotic and befitting of my *ĝha.*

Placing a hand to my chest, I say, "Mekho."

"Mex-ho," She repeats, raising a single eyebrow in my direction. My smile grows, and I tilt my horns to the right.

"Yes. Mekho."

"Mekho."

I want to hum in pleasure as she says my name. She got it right easily, regardless of the language barrier. My name on her lips has a drugging effect on me. Better than any *gingi leaf* I've ever had. I want to hear her say it again and again, preferably with her beneath me as I fill her with my –

"Aym naht goh-eeng whith yu. Wehr-eva yur goh-eeng, Mekho. *G'ú hì,* Mekho." *No go, Mekho.*

I can't help but smile because of her sweet words begging me not to go. Crossing the room to my *ĝha*'s seat at the Valkarran desk, I kneel before her. She does not stop me, though she seems wary as I take her supple hands in mine, untangling her folded arms. Staring deeply into her eyes, I make her a promise I know I could never break.

"I won't go anywhere without you, My Jewel. Never again."

Chapter Six
Priscille

The alien pirate, Mekho – I have to remember his name – is still kneeling in front of me as I pinch my eyes closed. *Your will be done, God. Is this your will?* I hold my breath in the silence, listening for His still, small answer. My lungs burn, and I accept this is His answer. But I don't like it. His will is whatever this pirate's is, it seems. Slowly releasing my breath, I open my eyes.

Gosh, he's beautiful. His cool gray eyes are pointed at me. His voice was so earnest when he said he would go nowhere without me. I melted a little. Then, he took my hands in his, and now he's giving me his undivided attention. I haven't had a man's attention like this since my last attempt at a summer fling. And the way that ended…

"Where's Serkha?" I ask, "The captain?"

He tilts his horns to the left in obvious confusion. "Not Serkha. Mekho."

I nod, understanding where the breakdown is and trying to find a solution. Mekho needs to understand my words as well as I understand his. He needs a translation bud. Looking around Serkha's office, I wonder if Blossom sent any extras – if Blossom even had any extras. But there are none on Serkha's desk, and Mekho won't release my hands long enough for me to search around.

"Priscille," he whispers. My body reacts before I do, turning back to him and meeting his gaze. His eyes search mine for something, and I realize what I must do. Yanking one hand from his, I remove the bud from my ear. I don't allow myself to overthink as I tilt his chin to the side and twist it into his ear. He is startled by my brash handling skills, but when I speak, those gray eyes fly wide.

"Where is Serkha? The captain of *this* ship?"

He's so stunned to understand my words that he seems frozen in place. Using my hand to tilt his chin down, I press my forehead against his and block out the other distractions in the room.

"Where is Serkha? My ship's captain?" I repeat.

"*Tú tà chiv ˆù.*"

Right. Only one of us gets to understand at a time. I pluck the earbud from Mekho's ear and stick it back in mine. Using my hands, I try to get him to say it again.

"She's with the crew."

I pull out the tiny bud again, offering it to him on my palm. This time, he takes it from me gently, placing it comfortably in his ear.

"Where is the crew? I want you to know I'm not going with you."

His brows furrow much deeper at those words now that he can understand me. But he pulls the tiny bud out of his ear and offers it back to me. He rests his arms on the sides of the chair, gently caressing my sides as I replace the bud.

It feels like a sin to like it. His easy intimacy should make me uncomfortable, but it doesn't. It only makes me want more. I want to cuddle up to him, rub on him like a cat or something. It makes me feel weak and makes me wonder why on Earth I ever wanted to be a nun.

When the earbud is secure, his face softens. "Your entire crew, the captain included, is safe, My Jewel. But if you do not agree to go with me, I cannot guarantee it will stay that way. Do you understand?"

Anger floats through me, and I go to remove the bud, but he stops me. Would he really manipulate me into leaving the only people I know on this entire planet? *Would he hurt them?* His hand holds me still, not allowing me to remove the bud and ask.

"I just need a tilt of agreement, Priscille. If you agree to come with me, willingly, then I will leave the crew as they are. On my honor."

What is the honor of a pirate worth anyway?

His hand wraps my wrist to keep me still, and my anger grows further. He's being gentle, but I still want to slap him around and force him to listen.

I can't abandon Serkha, who has been trying so hard to help me. Nor go with a pirate, not knowing if I'll ever see Clara again. I can't go with the man because he wants me to, because he makes me feel some kind of way.

"You must rid yourself of the anger, Priscille." Abbess Carlow whispers within my mind. When I'd spoken with Father Harvey about my sins, he had said the same thing. He said I needed to release my anger because it would cause me to sin. Yet, releasing anger was easier said than done. Forgiveness was not a path of little resistance.

Looking up at the man's pleading face, I take a deep breath and tilt my head to the right in agreement.

Chapter Seven

Mekho

My relief is instant. The tiny bean allows me to understand my *ĝha*'s words. It is incredible, but I have no interest in hearing her protests. If she is afraid to leave the Valkarran ship, then she will simply need to meet the women of my crew. It will help her feel more comfortable. They are just as kind and understanding as Serkha, I'm certain.

They accepted me as a captain, though a male captain is nearly unheard of. Ships and exploration were never made for men – a belief I had been silently feeling as of late. So, when she nodded her head to the right in acquiescence, it was time to go.

"Come with me, Priscille. I will introduce you to the others."

She takes my hand gently as if she does not want to hold onto me too tight. For fear of... Well, I do not understand her fear. Tightening my grip on her hand, I lead her out of the captain's quarters and toward the main mast. The sun is bright on the water, and it takes a moment for my eyes to adjust, but when I do, I am pleased.

We tied the crew of the Valkarran ship to the mast. Now, they glare in my direction as I lead my *ĝha* out of the chamber and into the sunshine. The Rough Waters beyond churn, which I note. It means we have little time before they become impassable. So, I must urge Priscille to be quick with her goodbyes. It was something I could do to soothe the transition.

"We must go quickly, but you may say goodbye to the crew and captain of this vessel," I explain, escorting her to the mast.

"Filthy pirate," the captain spits at me, disgust lacing her words. Though her eyes soften when she sees

Priscille. I only send her a winning smirk, releasing my *ĝha*'s hand so she can say her goodbyes.

My *ĝha* does not hesitate in her approach. The moment she sees the sapphire woman, she throws herself forward, wrapping her arms around the Valkarran. My Jewel sees the many ropes binding the crew and turns a glare in my direction, but after fumbling with them for only a few moments, her bound friends tell her they are fine. I know they will be let free soon enough.

Priscille tries to speak in a low voice to the captain, but My Treasure is not made to be silent. Her words reverberate as she speaks, and they bring light to those around her. She sparkles inside and out. Even if I do not understand her words.

"Hee whill naht hahrm yu, if aye goh."

Her old captain glares at me momentarily before smiling at my *ĝha*. She speaks in our native tongue, confirming my *ĝha* can understand us with the tiny bean she keeps in her ear. "You do not have to go with him, Priscille. We will suffer the consequences to keep you safe."

"Noh. Too hahv yu reesk yur lyf iz too muhch too ahsc, aye cewdnt. Teyll Clara, aye luv hrr."

"As you wish, Priscille. My honor as a woman says I must respect your wishes."

Serkha says these things as she glares in my direction. The woman clearly cares for my *ĝha*, and if I were not a pirate, I would thank her for the care she's given my *ĝha*. But unfortunately, the Rough Waters were churning, and we needed to go.

My *ĝha* does not waste more time speaking with her captain. She simply nods, wrapping her hands around the woman's horns before turning back to me. There is a set determination in her eyes, and I feel my hearts beat faster at the view.

I've seen many beautiful things in my travels across Shojo. Beautiful skies painted by Baso Sheva, whipping and wild storms, the beautiful spark of the *korovò* and their wisdom in my mind. Yet none were as captivating as my *ĝha* with determination in her eyes as she walked towards me. Her bountiful hips swing, and they could hypnotize me if I'm not careful.

"Your ship?" She asks in broken Vòllø, pointing as she speaks.

I tilt my horns to the right, trying to keep my grinning to a minimum. I am overjoyed that Priscille knows any of our words, but I cannot show her. My *ĝha* doesn't seem to love my happiness, but I love hers.

"Lower a plank," I order Kovi, offering a hand to my *ĝha* to help her across the way. She has clearly been on the water long enough to develop some sea legs, but she still walks like a baby *g `eĝiĉhœ*.

When she does not take my hand, I allow her the opportunity to try on her own. I am only two steps behind her.

With her arms out wide, she makes it about halfway across the plank before a wave rocks the ships. She tries to correct herself, her arm swinging through the air as she attempts to force her foot down. And she manages it. Not realizing her foot is on the plank, she overcorrects and goes tumbling.

Luckily, I'm quick on my feet. I catch Priscille by her side and scoop her into my arms, keeping my own feet moving across the plank beneath me. I hop onto the deck of my own ship, and I'm filled with a sense of coming home. As my *ĝha* stares up at me, wide-eyed, I know I'm closer than ever to finding my place in this world.

Chapter Eight
Priscille

I'm beginning to think Abbess Carlow was right. Prayer really is my only solace.

The moment we hit Mekho's deck, he has me escorted to the captain's cabin by two woefully anti-feminist Vòllø women. They don't seem to care that I don't want to be here. Or that holding me in the captain's cabin was the worst thing they could do to me. I plead with them, and I plead with God, to no avail. I'm shoved into the room and directed onto his bunk before they sheepishly close the door.

"This is ridiculous," I mutter, searching for something I can use – an escape, a weapon, or some other divine answer to my newest problems. Or any answer to any problem.

Mekho's cabin differs from Serka's. Cleaner, brighter, *bigger,* but just as humid. As I look around, I swipe the sweaty curls off the back of my neck and thank God for the braid, keeping my hair manageable. Two solid paned windows, made of actual glass, are wide and shallow at the back of the room, carving lines in the dust and lighting the space. His desk is completely free of clutter, but maps are tacked up on every spare inch of wall space. The whole room smells like him, like dark rum and something herbaceous.

Then, there's the bed. Four massive woven chain ropes hang on a bed big enough for three, allowing it to rock with the waves like my bunk on the other ship. It's layered with thin linens and colorful blankets, and stacks of pillows lean against the headboard attached to the back. The mattress itself is soft under my aching body.

Note to self: hitting the mast hurts.

Serkha had a simple hammock-style bed stuffed with comforting linen blankets and feather-stuffed pillows. But this bed was nothing like that. Running a hand over the duvet, I'm shocked at the softness of the material. It feels like my bamboo sheets at home, and if the bed didn't belong to a pirate, I would stay in it, curling up beneath the covers and sleeping away my pains. But, as it stood, those were dangerous thoughts. It didn't matter how incredibly inviting the thing was; it belonged to a man who wanted something from me, so I couldn't enjoy it.

Physically crawling away from temptation, I am surprised to find a prayer mat beneath the windows, similar to the ones in Wupeso. There are a couple of familiar runes marked into the wall before it and a tiny collection of crystals in every color of the rainbow. Art of a young maiden is drawn on sheets of paper and tacked to the floor.

Kneeling on the mat, I inspect the drawing curiously. It's obviously Baso Sheva, or part of the triplicate goddess anyway. She holds a curious orb in one hand and has a youthful, or maybe divine, glow around her. Brushing my hand across her visage, I feel the prickle of something 'other.' Yanking my hand away, I make the sign of the cross before folding them in front of me and closing my eyes to pray.

My parents were Catholic my whole life, but not the type that went to church often or attended a regular confessional. So, when I became so 'troubled,' as my mother called it — since, you know? Moving back in with your parents is so troubling — the obvious answer was for us all to turn to faith. They began bringing me to mass every Sunday and confessional once a week. I don't know when I decided the obvious choice was to become a nun, but suddenly, my life was full of prayer and study and learning how to take my vows.

At first, it was an easy way to escape my mother's questions for an hour or two. And I loved the idea of never having to remarry. Over time, it turned into something my father called 'the nun-run,' and I was visiting abbeys across the country to find the right sisterhood or cloister for me.

Right before I left for space, I was cloistered away on a temporary basis. That's where I met Abbess Carlow. She agreed to host me as a guest, and as a result, my traditional catholic prayers became ingrained in my soul. Now, I could use them to stabilize my mind, which I do now.

"Our Father, who art in heaven, hallowed be Thy name. Thy kingdom come, Thy will be done, on earth..." I pause. Taking a deep breath, I skip the rest. "In the name of the Father, and of the Son, and of the Holy Spirit. Amen."

My eyes flick open, and I'm greeted with the view of the drawings and crystals and slivers of light creeping through the windows above me. I'm reminded again that I'm not on Earth, and I don't know the spiritual protocol. I wasn't even a nun yet.

Then, my supposed *ĝha* walks into the room, and I'm even more confused. Mekho smiles in my direction, acting like this is totally normal. He's not even a little concerned about having me in his space as he strips out of his boots and tosses his shirt across the back of his desk chair. I suddenly feel flushed and try to blame the humidity in the room and not the shirtless alien man with beautiful tattoos up and down his carved chest.

I hate that he instantly turns me into a panting mess, and I turn away from him to continue cataloging the room. I'm on a prayer mat, for Christ's sake.

He pays me no mind, sitting at his desk and pulling open drawers. I monitor him through my peripheral as I search for a latch on the tiny windows. My lower body would never fit through them, so I can't escape, but at least they could let in a breeze. Unfortunately, there wasn't a latch at all, so it didn't matter in the end.

Walking along each wall, I locate an armoire. Maybe if I were snoopy enough, the pirate would realize what a mistake it was to leave me in here unsupervised. Maybe he would decide I was too much trouble and throw me in a brig instead.

Opening the door to the armoire, I glance over my shoulder, but Mekho simply smirks down at his paperwork as I rifle through it. Mostly, it's just stuffed with extra clothes, some blue liquid in a colored glass bottle, and books bound with leather. Pulling one from the bottom of the armoire, I find a seat on the floor and open it.

I arrange my skirts around me and look at the simplistic language. Since Vera married Kano back in Wupeso, the women and children had been learning about the Vòllø cultures. We learned about the Vòllø language of the islands and how they wrote. There were runes for certain items, especially tradeable ones. In these books, I saw some I understood, like fish and wood and fruit. Then, there were the runes I didn't understand, which made up many of the pages.

The runes curved beautifully from a central mark, with the wavy, hatched numbers beneath to denote the measures of each item. If you were to imagine a grid, it would be like a honeycomb, each tiny hexagon holding a perfect record, spiraling out to the edges of each rustic page.

After my basic perusal, I try to note which runes repeat regularly to get an idea of what my *ĝha* might like to trade in. One tiny rune looked like the trees in Valkarra. It was common, and I knew it meant lumber, but they wrote those numbers on top of those runes, which led me to believe those were purchases. I assumed it was for ship repairs. In Serkha's ledgers, she only tracked sales since Valkarra did not import from the older tribe they traded with, and all her numbers had gone beneath her runes.

That's why I looked at the runes with the highest numbers beneath them.

Though I didn't understand all the runes, the Vòllø number system was simple. It was base-ten, like our human system, and the ones, tens, hundreds, and thousands markings were easy to distinguish and similar to a curvy Roman numeral. The numbers almost looked like human letters, lowercase l's, c's, k's, and x's. So, I noticed where those x's were and cataloged the runes beside them to ask about later.

Unfortunately, I became so engrossed in my study of a ledger I missed when my *ĝha* rose from his desk to come and study me instead of his maps. Truthfully, I had forgotten about his presence in the room. The level of comfort I had with him was unnerving.

"Rise, My Jewel. If you wish to know of our cargo, I'll show you."

His voice was smooth and buttery, and I cursed my lustful heart as I tilted my head back to meet Mekho's eyes. He held out one hand for me, his shirt haphazardly thrown over the opposite shoulder. Hardening my heart against the temptation of him, I huffed a sigh and pushed myself from the ground, ignoring his offered assistance.

I felt a little wobbly as I regained my sea legs, but when he reached out to stabilize me, I stepped back instead, gripping onto my skirts for balance. Dusting myself off, I tossed the book on the mattress behind him and tilted my head to the right in acquiescence.

"Show me."

Chapter Nine

Mekho

I loved to watch Priscille move. Her words were too foreign for my ears to understand without the help of her tiny ear thing, so I relied on what her body told me. The way she would nod her head before tilting it to the right seemed strange at first, but since I learned it meant agreement, I loved it. I also enjoyed watching her tiny hands. The maps had completely lost my attention when I saw her draw the tip of her finger across her tiny pink tongue and flip another page in the ledger. Now, I watched them flex as she fisted them in her skirts, lifting away the material to step onto the deck.

The crew was busy preparing to bring us across the Rough Waters once again, but she didn't seem to pay them any mind. Shielding her eyes from the sun, she glanced back at me before traipsing further into the fray.

My Treasure had no directional instinct as she walked on, curving around a set of barrels and stopping herself short before Niti could take off her head. I glared up at the tiny sailor, and she flicked her tail in my direction apologetically.

"Priscille," I said, motioning for her to come back towards me.

The deck was a dangerous place normally. Now, it was in disarray from the collision with the Valkarrans, and everything needed to be tied down and refreshed before we attempted the deep, choppy waters again.

It's not that I wanted to face the Rough Waters with my *ĝha* aboard my ship, but taking the long way around to the other port would be equally treacherous. We could run into the Valkarrans again after they visit the old tribal land, and they may be in better spirits. Or worse, we could set upon some of the old water beasts the older tribes train to kill. The absolute worst scenario: the mainlanders find us before I can sneak into their crystal fields. The Rough Waters were no more dangerous than the grueling journey ahead if we took the way around them.

My *ĝha* is not quick to follow my obvious command. Instead, she searches for another way forward before realizing she has trapped herself between working women and the mess they are trying to tame. With a huff of breath, she walks back toward me, ignoring my offered hand once again. *If I were a less civilized man, it would drive me to madness.*

Instead of allowing her to continue to lead us through messes, I match her stride and direct her through the fray and to the hatch leading to the belly of the ship. She pauses there, looking at me as if I might lead her to her death.

Opening the grate, I am dramatic in my encouragement, sweeping my arms down toward the hole to indicate she should go through. Her eyes are full of wariness when they flash toward me, so, dropping my smirk, I motion for her to follow me and slip down the tiny rope ladder.

When I say My Treasure is a curious creature, I mean it both in her capacity for curiosity and the curiosity she inspires in me. Deep in the ship's belly, I can see our large lumber containers and newly formed barrels, but she seems to squint into the shadows. It is a reminder that she is much weaker than my Vòllø crew, and I seek the glowing lantern we keep down here for the night hours. I am confident our earnings and organization will impress her once she can see it.

Opening the small glow lantern, soft gold light dances in fractals across the curved wood of my ship. The light allows her to see the soft pinkish tone of the wood while making the shadows seem even more foreboding.

"This way." I offer my arm to escort her through the cargo. When she ignores it again, it feels as though she wishes to slacken my sails. But I say nothing, holding onto the glowing light for her weak alien eyes instead.

Priscille picks up on the organizational format quickly, pointing out the words and numbers written in ink char on the outside of each box without me telling her. When she realizes the overall themes – perishables, non-perishables, legal, not so legal – she smiles. It's as if she's discovered the secret door to Ubahina, the realm of Baso Sheva, where the fields of crystals bear fruit and illuminate the darkest parts of your soul. As she points to a box and asks me a question, I try to parse her stumbling words but ultimately end up pointing to my ears to explain I don't understand.

Understanding dawns on her immediately, and she pulls the tiny white thing from her ear before handing it to me. She's patient with me as I tuck it into my ear, and I hear a fuzzy crackle.

"What does this symbol mean?"

I peer at the dark markings half-hidden behind her and realize the tiny box she's picked out of the entirety of our cargo is the one I'd rather she not know about. Unfortunately, the box is so small, and she knows so many of the runes already it's hard to shuffle through my mind for a suitable lie. Luckily, she holds out her hand for the bud as I mumble through my excuses, giving me more time to think something up.

I land on "Special seeds."

She repeats the Vòllø word for seeds curiously and picks up the box, shaking it gently. Her eyes narrow in my direction, and I can feel my skin pale under her scrutiny. Serkha had said something about my *ĝha* wanting to be some kind of priestess on her last world, and with a look like that, she would have made a great one.

Pulling the box from her hand, I tucked the package behind me. She reaches for the box, but I grab her hand and twirl her into my chest. She stumbles slightly, but I don't let her fall, catching her with a bent knee for stabilization. My horns are parallel to the floor as I stare down at her. She's pressed against my chest as her sweet scent invades me. She smells like *r`ùlo°* flowers and a cool sea breeze. I can feel her tiny hand on my thigh, warm and tense as she scrambles upright.

I watch as she brushes down her skirts with one hand – something I've realized is a nervous tick of hers. One of many.

She stands tall, drawing her eyes up my chest to meet my gaze, and holds out her palm for the translation piece. My eyes flick to both of my hands, one still gripped tightly in hers and the other holding onto the small cargo box, before meeting her stare again. She follows my trail and gasps when she realizes our free hands are still tangled together, hanging between us.

It's almost painful letting her pull away from me. She snatches her hand back like I am a flame and shakes out her fingers as if they are smoking. Her brows furrow almost imperceptibly, and she shakes her head as if she needs to dislodge a wayward thought. Then, with one hand on her hip, she silently demands the tiny white thing from my ear.

Chapter ten
Priscille

After the weird excursion to the cargo bay, I was feeling antsy. It was like I was too big for my skin, and I wanted to crawl out of it, all while being stuffed into a ten-by-ten room under lock and key. Mekho didn't come in after me, and for some reason, that made it worse. Instead, he left me with a parting shot – a meaningful look at the bed, followed by a downright lusty look at me. I was practically hyperventilating by the time I heard the lock click behind him.

At first, I tried to pray, but once again, I was tempted away. I couldn't think in my state of stillness or long enough to recall practiced words or pleas of my own. So, I paced instead, murmuring under my breath for whichever deity would hear me. Staring down at a woven rug beneath me, I worried I would walk the color right out of it and forced myself to sit on the edge of the bed.

Glancing at the windows toward the back of the ship, I could see the sun setting in the distance. My first night in the captain's quarters would begin soon. The panic was setting in.

On Serkha's ship, I slept with the crew. There were hammock bunks, and I was toward the center of the stacks, on the bottom bunk. A woman with lavender hair slept above me and did my braids every morning, even though she couldn't understand my babbling. The only things we knew about one another were names and sleeping habits. Her name was Ikana, and she was so silent when she slept I would hover my hand beneath her hammock to ensure her body was still warm sometimes. She called me Prissy instead of Priscille, oblivious to the connotations held on Earth, and she knew I snored like a woman with a deviated septum. Likely because I was a woman with a deviated septum.

Pulling myself together, I pressed my palms firmly against one another in front of me and took five deep breaths. That practice wasn't one my parents gave me. In fact, it was my sixth-grade teacher. Some group of kids had called me ugly, a usual insult among their repertoires. They said the way I looked was a sin; it was a *funny* catholic school joke, and I couldn't handle it that day. I ran away crying and found a deep, dark hallway to hide in.

Then, Miss Padinski, a classic beauty with blond hair, blue eyes, and a proportionally hourglass figure, came after me. I'd heard the other girls call her Lady Love and Light before, but when she arrived in the hallway to speak softly with me and remind me of my value, she was like an angel in the dark. I understood exactly what they meant. The cruel shadows of the hallway seemed to dissolve behind her, warded away by the click of her heeled boots.

She didn't care about the dust as she kneeled in front of me or the snot running down my face. For a few moments, she simply breathed loudly, in a calm cycle, until I stopped hiccupping for breaths of my own. Then, she offered me a tissue from the colorful package in her pocket. I cleaned my face and tucked away the evidence of my meltdown before she pressed my hands together for me and taught me the breathing technique.

When I was finally calm, she told me I was beautiful and we all brought value to the world. It was refreshing, so unlike the religious guilt I would develop later, that the practice I attached to her words stuck, even during my time visiting the abbey and before joining the women on the way out of the escape pod.

Unfortunately, the effects didn't last when the door to the captain's cabin opened, and Mekho was standing there. His signature grin was plastered to his face, and he held two wooden bowls in one hand. Citrusy, spicy steam filled the room with its scent, and my stomach growled angrily. It immediately reminded me I hadn't eaten that day.

My innate desire for food completely overwrote my intentions of keeping my distance from the handsome pirate. I met him at the desk and stole the bowl from him, sipping down some of the fragrant broth. I was unprepared for the instant heat, both in temperature and spice, but I swallowed it down anyway, ignoring the burn in my throat. As far as I could taste, it was delicious. Some kind of cross between chamoy and the original flavor of ramen.

Tilting the bowl away from my face, I set it on the table, feeling a drip of the broth slide down my chin. Before I could catch it, Mekho was there. His callused thumb brushed up my chin and across my bottom lip to catch the droplet. The heated look he gave me before he left the room earlier was back with a vengeance. Pulling his thumb away from my lip, he pushes the wayward broth between his lips and hums with pleasure.

The world seems to spin when he steps away from me, but since that happens every time he leaves my vicinity, I'm becoming used to it. It's like when he's in my orbit, the gravitational pull changes, and when he leaves, it has to recalibrate again. This time, I was ready. My hand reached for the extra chair behind his desk. It both stabilized me and gave me a place to sit and eat.

Mekho took the spot across the desk, the captain's chair, and pulled a wilted leaf from his bowl, slurping it down like a noodle.

Using my double-tined spork, I followed his lead. The glossy green leaves were delicious; obviously, the food that gave the broth its citrusy flavor felt bright and fresh.

Next, I picked out a tiny blue kernel and a few grains of the *llige* I was familiar with. I expected it to taste like corn, but it tasted similar to a mango, light and sweet but with an unfamiliar texture. It definitely wasn't my favorite part of the soup, but I finished the bowl anyway.

Then, I cursed myself for eating so quickly when I realized what came next.

The looming threat of the bed was now imminent. As Mekho took my bowl from me, he asked if I was full. I wanted to lie, but I didn't. Just because I wasn't sure my prayers were being heard didn't mean I would sin left and right. Another look at the bed had me tense, but if we only slept, it couldn't be a sin, right? The point being, I gave him the nod-tilt to let him know I was plenty full. The soup satisfied me, without my usual craving for something sweet right after it.

After he set them aside, he stripped out of his shirt, walking to the armoire I'd rifled through earlier. I felt heat rise to my cheeks at all his bare skin, and I tried not to trace the lines of his back with my eyes. Stripping out of his pants, I snapped my head away, focusing on the lack of moon outside the windows. I could still hear churning water beneath the boat, but without the light of day, I had only the stars to show me where the sea ended and the sky began.

"For you," Mekho murmured, proud of his use of human language. He handed me one of his shirts from the armoire.

I don't know what I expected. I refused to tell Mekho where my things were on Serkha's ship, so we had moved nothing of mine over with me. If he had been holding onto something for an ex-lover, that would have been upsetting too. So, with shaking hands, I took the shirt from him. I waited for him to turn around, but when he didn't, I did. Giving him my back, I stripped the top of my gown before hastily slipping the shirt over myself.

One bright side I found to being claimed by an alien his size was his shirt actually fit like a nightdress. It grazed the tops of my thighs, and the wrists hung well past my hands. It was something I had never experienced on Earth, even in my two serious relationships, before pursuing becoming a nun. Both relationships were with guys a few inches shorter than me. One was skinnier than a bean pole, and the other was fairly athletic, but neither one of them could have lent me their shirt as a night dress.

Rolling up the sleeves to my wrists, I tighten the strings at my neck and check that I'm decent before turning back to the bed.

I have always been a bigger girl. I skipped sizes zero through twelve when I became a teenager, and from the time I turned fourteen, my stomach became a softened little pouch no number of crunches could take away from me. Shapewear and I were close friends, at least until I gave up all my vanity and tried to become a nun. Then, I decided there were more important things than how my body looked. How I treated my body became the more important thing to me.

Unfortunately, I couldn't help the slight nervousness that the massive alien with lusty eyes would see my dimpled thighs and run for the hills.

I drag my eyes up to the bed, preparing for the worst. Mekho reclines on the pillow, an arm propping up his head so he can watch me as I fidget. He's shirtless, with all his ropy muscles on display. The bicep propping up his head flexes, making my mouth water, and his other veiny forearm rests across his lower abs. A body like sin, my mother would have said.

Luckily for me, he's lying on top of the covers, and he doesn't move to touch me when I come to stand on the side he's not occupying.

"Come to bed," He urges, leaning over to my side. He drags the blankets out of my way, patting the perfect space between the clean sheets before resuming his position of perfect relaxation.

I nibble on my bottom lip, unease dripping through me. Right now, the pirate acts as if I will be alone beneath the sheets. He's being kind and patient, but I know what men are like. What if he expects something from me I can't give him?

Ripping the earbud out of my ear, I shove it in his direction. His brows furrow, but he is quick to take it from me, putting it in his ear.

"We're not having sex." I blurt. I slap my hand to my mouth immediately, feeling my eyebrows shoot to my hairline. Mekho only smirks until his sweet smile turns into a full-belly laugh. Yet, it's not a threatening one. It's not like he's laughing at me because I'm so laughably wrong. It's like he's laughing at me because I was concerned he would take advantage of me or something. Like anyone here would take advantage of me.

He offers me back the earbud, and I know I'm blushing when I stick it back in my ear.

In that candy voice of his, he whispers, "No, My Treasure. We are not having sex tonight. In fact, I will sleep above the covers for your comfort. It is obvious you will need time to acclimate to me, and I am happy to take my time with you."

Though his words are reassuring, I can still feel their heat. There's an undertone in his last statement. He's happy to take his time with me – winning me, owning me, loving me. I stifle a shiver and climb beneath the sheets.

Mekho treats me like an abused puppy, moving slowly as he tucks the sheets around me gently. Then, he deliberately goes slower when he lowers his lips to my forehead and places a kiss there.

The day was long, and I'm not surprised to find I have no trouble getting to sleep. I thought maybe I would be worried with Mekho watching over me like a hawk, but having his eyes on me helped. As he whispered, "Goodnight," it was like I finally felt safe.

Chapter Eleven
Mekho

Navigating the Rough Waters twice in one day had me feeling like my luck had run thin. But then I ate dinner with Priscille in my cabin and convinced her to sleep in my bed. Now, I was convinced she was my good luck charm. I would never sail another day without her. And now that she was asleep, I could not go another minute without thanking Vova.

Sneaking out of bed, I find a comfortable position on my prayer mat before whispering my prayers. My mother had taught me the most faithful prayers were said aloud and that we must always keep one in our hearts. Now, Baso Sheva had answered my greatest hearts' prayer, and I owed her one aloud.

Before the ship was mine, it was my mother's. But she died of old age, years before the Death of Baso Sheva, when I was still a mere boy. The crew wanted to toss me to sea to be with her or drop me at the next most convenient port. But Kovi convinced them I could be a good deckhand. Then, she taught me everything she knew, on top of all my mother had taught me, and when I came of age, she announced me captain of the ship that had been my only home. That was many seasons ago now, but I remained grateful.

"Vova, grant me an audience, for I have much to be grateful for this night," I murmur, checking over my shoulder. Relief fills me to see the steady rise and fall of my *ĝha*'s chest.

Under my breath, I continue, "Thank you for your protection over the Rough Waters, for the blessing of my *ĝha*, for her place here on my ship. Please forgive my hastiness with the Valkarrans and bless their travels.

Please solve our issue of language as you have for many others."

I pause again, peeking over my shoulder and lowering my voice further. In the barest of whispers, I vow, "Wherever she wants to go, I will go with her. You've given me a home, and I will never leave it. *D'o go chu merchu.*"

After my prayers of devotion are through, I stand from my mat, cursing a small creak in the floor as I creep back toward the bed. However, every time I look at my *ĝha*, she is still breathing evenly as she sleeps. Since she is so restful, I take a peek at my star-maps and our charted course, ensuring all is well before sneaking back to bed.

Once I am securely in my place, confident my *ĝha* still sleeps, I relax into a position where I can study her face. When awake, My Treasure is a constant trove of human reactions. Her brows move about her face as if they are completely unattached; her color changes from the pale color it normally holds to a fresh red like coals and flame. She has no *jisa* to protect her, so instead of it shuddering or collapsing, her skin develops tiny bumps to ward against unfamiliar chills. Every little thing is so interesting to my eye when she is awake. The way her mouth moves, and the different shapes it makes when she tries to speak the Vòllø language rather than her human one, the way her nose wrinkles at an unpleasant smell. It is all a vast, overwhelming codex to her inner experience, and I want to read it all.

Yet, while she sleeps, she does none of this. While she sleeps, her face is completely relaxed. Her lips are softly parted, and the soft rise and fall of her chest is a rhythmic sort of lullaby.

At least until she draws in some kind of special breath and a startling rumble and wheeze shudders in and out of her perfect body. My curiosity drags me closer as she

47

takes another one of these special breaths, and I am surprised to realize she is snoring. My smile grows slowly, widening as another loud and rousing snore escapes the slight curve of her lips. I want to laugh, but I have no desire to wake her. So, I stifle it in my pillow as I realize she may wake the whole crew.

I can barely comprehend the juxtaposition of my perfect treasure and her loud sleeping sounds, but somehow, I adore them, and they lull me to sleep anyway.

Chapter Twelve

Priscille

After a great night's rest, I feel more prepared to continue my original mission. I went with Serkha to find the spiritual answers I needed, and all I found was a *ĝha* of my own. Not very befitting of a nun, if I so say so myself. I listen for Abbess Carlow's voice in my head, confirming my suspicions, but she is silent as I dress for the day and fix my braids. The braids don't look nearly as nice as Ikana's work, but they'll do.

When I'm finally ready for the day, I go to the door to the deck and find it... locked. I jiggle the handle a little and try to pull it open, but it doesn't come open, no matter how hard I try.

Mekho left over an hour ago, dropping another kiss on my forehead while I was still half-asleep. Now that I was ready to join him, the door wouldn't even open. Worse, my bladder was becoming a burgeoning issue, and my stomach was threatening to grumble louder than my snores.

Knocking on the door politely, I dance from one foot to the next, waiting for someone to come help me. On Serkha's ship, they had an awful privy swing thing that scared me so bad the fear had me finding relief. I figured this would be the case here as well, but if no one came to open this door, the rug would become my privy instead. After several minutes of no answer, I bang on the door a little louder. *Maybe they didn't hear me.*

"Hello! Can someone let me out to pee?"

I felt ridiculous screaming that into the ether, but I needed attention stat. Mekho was the one keeping me like a caged pet, leaving me in his *locked* office so I couldn't roam the deck and run off into the vast, never-ending, alien ocean. As if I would.

"Hello!" I call again, slamming my fist into the door. "Come on! Someone help me."

Suddenly, the lock clicks, and I have to hop back to avoid the swinging door.

It's not Mekho, but a burly sort of woman with blue skin the same shades of the ocean. I want to strangle the part of me that's disappointed it's not Mehko – because it's simply too early to feel that way about my captor – but I'm too relieved to see a face; I don't even care it's not a happy one.

Speaking slowly, I say, "I have to pee. Restroom. Swing thing." I point to the downstairs area, ignoring my embarrassment for a bathroom break, and give her a pleading smile.

Her brows furrow and she says nothing as she slams the door closed and locks it in place once again.

"Wait! Help!" I shout, banging on the door immediately. It was becoming a Code Red fast, and I didn't want my next helper to ignore my pleas. If I didn't get out of here, I would have to sacrifice Mekho's rug and my dignity, all in one fell swoop.

Then, the door swung open, and a very startled Mekho was standing there in all his glory. He was carrying some kind of food, and as delicious as it looked, I was going to explode. Thrusting the earbud at him, I practically shout, "I need to pee."

I'm glaring up at him, waiting for him to move, but he seems frozen in the doorway. Then, as if by the power of God, my words finally register. Half-walking, half-sprinting across the deck, he directs me to where I need to be.

"You can go now." I grumble, "I'll come find you once I'm done."

With a tilt of his horns, I finally get my moment of privacy.

After breakfast, it becomes clear I am still a prisoner, but I am at least a prisoner who has made my needs known. Once every few hours, I'm brought out of the captain's cabin for a walk across the deck to use the bathroom, and I'm offered food and snacks. It's as if I'm some kind of pet.

That is exactly what I tell Mekho the next time he comes through.

He's sitting in my room with a midday meal when I return from my third walkabout of the day — not that I need many, but I take the opportunities for the fresh air. He smiles at me, and I try to be Christ-like and not glare in his direction. *Father, forgive me my sins.* Mekho still has the earbud because he never returned it after the debacle...

"I'm not a dog, you know," I said, immediately tucking into my food. The pirate chews thoughtfully, and I wonder if they have dogs here. Vera had a massive dragon beast thing, and I saw plenty of wildlife in Valkarra but few pets and certainly no dogs. "And even if I were one, walking across the ship every three hours isn't a solution for my care. You need to give me some freedom."

I watch him chew carefully. His lip tilts up in the smirk of his that drives me to rage, and I promise myself I'll pray for forgiveness on my knees the moment he leaves. He hands me the earbud.

"You are safest in here."

"I am locked in here," I reply, cursing myself because he cannot understand my words. Handing him the earbud, I force myself to repeat my words.

He immediately hands the earbud back, his smile still strong on his face.

"There is an easy way to gain all the freedom you wish," He explains, taking a slow bite of his food.

The food is superb today. On Serkha's ship, it was all the same stuff we ate in Valkarra but kept cold in ice boxes and never fresh. On Mekho's ship, the food seemed almost made to order. We ate some things warm, some cold, but all of it was fresh and delicious. It made arguing with the arrogant alien more difficult.

"Explain," I say, motioning with my hands for him to go on. He swallows his bite, setting down his utensil and meeting my gaze.

"Vova gives with a fickle hand. If we were to join, I would know for certain this is real. Vova could not steal it like precious cargo.

"In three sun cycles, we will be at a port where a *r̈uṣad'ù* could be held. If you promise to join with me, then I will give you the freedom you wish."

We pass the earbud back and forth as we speak.

"On Earth, my home planet, I promised never to take a husband – or I planned to anyway," I pause, not completely capable of looking him in the eye. "I made a promise to my God. He sustains the existence of the entire universe, so I must keep my promise to Him."

The bit about the universe is something I heard one sister say to someone during our escape from the *SS Herculean*. She was trying to explain that even though we were so far from Earth, we could still follow God's plan. When I knew I would be returning to Earth, that seemed easy enough to accept, but now, my faith was shaken.

"If your God rules the entire universe, then surely he knows Baso Sheva. Surely they collaborate to see your God's plan come to life."

"It sounds like you're telling me 'everything happens for a reason.'"

"Does it not?"

We ate in silence for a few moments as I pondered his words. It was something I had considered since landing here. My relationship with God had never been as strong as others, which was an exceedingly worrisome thing for me as I pursued my path to the nunnery, but even more so now that I did not have the faith of others to lean on. With my prayers cast seemingly into the void and no soft, holy voice whispering back at me, the existence of Baso Sheva seemed like the obvious path. From my study in Wupeso and Valkarra and my talks with Kano and the temple priestesses, I knew that looked like accepting a *ĝha*, praying among the crystals, giving glory to Baso Sheva. My problem was that my obvious path was as believable as the theory where I died on the *SS Herculean* and was cast into hell for my sins.

Maybe only the devil had a voice like chocolate peanut butter candies.

With a sigh, I ask, "What would my freedom look like?"

"If we were bound by a holy *r̈ uṣad'ù*, it could look however you wished, My Jewel."

"And if I wish to go back to Valkarra?"

"I would ask you to pick a different place."

"Wupeso, then. There are more human women there. I could be with my people."

"And me," He explains, offering me a glass of fresh water. I tilt my head to the right and take a sip as I consider his words.

"As long as I didn't have to live on a ship for the rest of my life. Or be without the other human women. I have a best friend in Valkarra; I would visit her often – whether or not you joined me."

"Does this mean you agree to the *r¨uṣad'ù*?"

"No. I have to think about it. Pray about it." I finish my food, but I'm still feeling unsatisfied. Glancing at Mekho, his eyes soften, and he tilts his head to let me know he understands. Then, he slides his bowl across the table and pulls a wrapped sweet cake from his pocket. The gesture is so kind my heart melts, even as he stands from his chair.

Sun streams through the crack in the door, but he pauses before he leaves.

"As soon as you agree to the *r¨uṣad'ù*, freedom is yours, Treasure."

Chapter Thirteen

Mekho

I had Kovi bring dinner to Priscille, and I slept with the crew to give her time to think; even though every fiber of my being wanted me to go sleep beside her and be the one to take her around the ship, I knew she wouldn't appreciate that. She needed time to pray, meditate with her God, and listen for an answer. I did not want to intervene or make her feel pressured. No matter how much I already loved my *ĝha*, if she did not want me, that was her choice.

This did not stop me from thinking about her constantly. As I helped work the ropes and guide the ship, I imagined her reading my ledgers. Her knees tucked close as she leaned against the wall of my cabin. Her eyes focused on the tiny scripts as she tried to teach herself the words she was too stubborn to ask about. Then, when I found my way to bed, I imagined her precious face. The tiny upward turn of her nose as her grinding, growling snores tore out of her. Without them, it was already hard to fall asleep. Now, the first sliver of the sun was barely approaching the horizon, and I could not sleep a wink longer without seeing her.

Climbing from my cot, I sneak silently from the bunks and back to my cabin.

I open the door to find my *ĝha*. Her feet are crossed beneath her on the bed. A glow crystal lantern sits beside her as she flips another page of the ledger. She's taken her hair out of her tight braids, and it falls down her back in warm waves while the shorter pieces at the front slip into her line of sight. My Treasure wears my shirt, and the sight brings a pleasant warmth to my chest. She's so engrossed in what she's doing that she doesn't even notice me. Not as I step in or when I close the door, but when I climb onto the bed, she looks up at me with a jerk.

"Mekho."

"Priscille," I offer her my hand. She eyes it shrewdly, looking between the ledger and my hand as if she can't decide which choice is scarier. Then, she takes my hand.

I lead her out of the room to the bow of the ship, placing her in front of me and guiding her hands to the railing. The morning air on the sea is chilled, but I keep my body close, letting my arms brush against hers and holding onto the rail beside her. Any moment now, the sun will crest the sea-line, and the green streak in the sky will fade.

"Wut ahr wee doh-ing owt hehr?" From our previous conversations, I've only been able to pick up a few words, but what was familiar enough that I knew she was asking a question – likely about why I dragged her out of bed. I curl closer to her until my lips brush her ear.

"Watch, Treasure."

Instead of protesting, she sighs, taking in the scene before her. The ethereal shade of purple, like the legendary crystal dunes, takes over the sky. When the first curve of the sun makes its appearance, its light scatters across the choppy waves, and the sea glistens in a golden hue. As the deep red of the night sky fades, and the sun makes its ascent, the discordant stripe of green moves its way down the skyline until it's buried by Vova in the sea.

As it all happened, I watched my *ĝha*. I saw her frustration dissolve as the beauty of a sea sunrise took her breath away. She stared forward, encased in the moment of peace. Though the air held a chill, the light of the sun warmed my *jisa* and highlighted all the perfect contours of my *ĝha*'s face. She folded her arms against the railing and rested her chin on them as she watched. I could have sworn I heard her whisper words of her faith, but when I leaned closer, she was silent.

Then, the ship began to bustle. Crew members emerged from the bunks below to find their places on the ship. Priscille didn't mind the noise. She simply turned in my arms, met my gaze, and said two words in Vòllø. *"R̈ u̥sad'ù. J è."*

Chapter Fourteen
Priscille

Mekho didn't lie when he said I would have complete freedom on the ship. After I told him I would go through with the ceremony, he held out his hand for the earbud and told me he would escort me back to the cabin to get dressed, and then I could spend the day as I wished. It was what I had hoped for, but the man was a pirate, so a small part of me was still surprised. Even more so when I twisted the handle of the captain's cabin, and it opened without issue.

Stepping onto the deck, freedom never felt so good. As I sauntered forward, Kovi was the first person to catch sight of me. Her eyes bugged out wide, and she immediately came to intercept me.

"*ẹ̆liqĕ ĝu va i˘ lu.*" She pointed to the captain's cabin door. I shake my head before remembering to follow it up with a head tilt, and her nostrils flare. She's obviously upset I'm not in my tiny cage, but I refuse to go back until I have to. A couple days trapped away from the sun, and there was nothing more blissful than feeling its warmth on my back.

"Take it up with Mekho," I explain, skirting around the big and beautiful pirate woman. Her hand comes around my upper arm a little too tight for my liking, and I try to pull it out. Fear slides into my veins, and another time of my life flashes before me.

For a moment, I'm no longer on Shojo but Earth. It's not a big alien pirate gripping my arm, but a man with unkempt facial hair and a smarmy grin. He's three drinks in, and I can smell the liquor on his breath, feel him tighten his grip on my arm as he forces me against the brick wall, his free fist winding back. *"This is your fault, Priscille. If you didn't want me to be angry, then –*

A hand comes down on my shoulder, and I jump even as Kovi's grip on my arm releases. Then, his hand brushes down my arm, and I let out a soft exhale. *All is well. All is well.* I assure myself of that as Mekho's hand tangles with my own. When I look up to him, I see anger on his face, but his hand is gentle in mine.

I tug on it slightly, pulling his attention to me. Knowing he has my earbud, I say, "It's okay. Everything is okay."

I can't tell if it's a tick or if he means things are not okay, but he half-growls as his horns tilt to the left. Handing me the earbud, he says, "Apologize to my *ĝha*, Kovi."

Though Kovi's eye color flashes wide and then narrow, she listens, "I am sorry for touching you, Lady Priscille."

"Now, make your rounds. Let the crew know Priscille can go wherever she wants and that they should all be friendly to her. She is my most esteemed guest."

Kovi gives a slight tilt of her horns before she disappears from the deck.

Mekho spins me around in his arms, stroking over the spot where Kovi gripped me so tight. Looking into his eyes, I can't help but feel slightly soothed, even if my mind is still running wild. He takes a knee before me so we're eye to eye, and my heart aches at the gesture.

I hadn't pondered August in a long time. Once everything with him ended, my time was consumed with visiting and volunteering at nunneries, speaking with my priest and family, and praying – day in and day out. Then, Abbess Carlow and my parents suggested the *SS Herculean,* and I ended up here. I continued the path I thought would absolve me, and I ended up in this man's arms.

Mekho's eyes are full of color, radiating concern toward me like a physical touch, but I can't explain this to him. Even if we were to pass the earbud back and forth, I'm not sure I would have the patience to explain. I felt too shaken to even breathe properly. Then, a fresh fear struck, sinking in like an anchor in quicksand. I had a past with August on Earth. If Mekho knew about it, would he still want me?

He must sense where my mind spirals to because his hands come to rest on both sides of my face, keeping my vision locked straight ahead, straight on him. When I close my eyes to avoid his gaze, a tear slips down my cheek. His thumb is warm as it grazes the salty droplet, brushing it away.

Mekho's touch is so tender it hurts. I almost wish he would be rougher with me just so I could catalog him with the men I knew before. But he never tightens his grip. He never forces me to look at him. He doesn't even growl out unintelligible demands or blame me for not understanding them.

My eyes burn hot, and stinging tears fall one after the other. All the while, I pray under my breath. "Lord be with me. Bless me with your strength. Soothe my frayed nerves. Lord, be with me, please. Help me to find solace."

"Priscille."

My eyes snap open, and Mekho's gaze is still full of concern, but it's gentle and understanding and completely pacifying. He tilts his head to the captain's cabin and asks in broken English, "To talk?"

Chapter Fifteen
Mekho

One morning on deck, My Jewel is already in tears. Something hurt her, and I was not there to stop it, proving to me I must bond her to me quickly so I can keep her safe.

She allows me to bring her back to my chambers, but I can tell she's not happy about it. I try to assure her I am not locking her up again by leaving the door cracked open, but she leans against me to push it closed herself. Then, pulling a blanket from the bed, she tucks it over her head and around her strong shoulders like a hooded cloak. She pads across the rug again and presses her body against mine.

My arms come around her naturally, and her subsequent sigh eases my tension. Without disconnecting from our embrace, she passes me the translation device.

"You probably want to know what that was all about, huh?" She whispers, peering up at me like I'm an executioner.

I tilt my horns in agreement but run a soothing hand over her back. No matter what my *ĝha* has to say, I will still adore her when this is through. I want her to know as much, even if I cannot say so without passing this tiny thing back and forth. Over the past few days with her on my ship, I have learned that Priscille is perfect for me. She has a curious mind, a faithful soul, and an impenetrable will. She would never allow me to flounder through tragedies as I have these past months, and she is an example to me in more ways than one.

She sighs again, stepping away from me. When I try to follow her, she shakes her head. It's a display of strength I admire.

"I need some space to talk about this," She explains, taking a steadying breath. "You may wish for a different *ĝha* after this."

"Never," I scoff, though she cannot understand me. I tilt my head with disagreement, slashing my tail across my heart. She's so wrong that I must work to keep my head. The primal part of me growls for me to show her exactly what I want, but my control won't allow me to succumb to those urges. I would never want to cause fear to Priscille, so I force myself to keep my distance.

Her fingers are white around the knuckles as she clings to the blanket, but her eyes are clear when she says, "For a time, I had a husband on Earth. A *ĝha* – sort of."

My teeth clenched on instinct, hearing her call another man her *ĝha*. A husband, a long-term mate she made promises to, sure, but he was certainly not her *ĝha*. From the way she holds herself and the way she speaks of him, I can tell as much. I force myself to ease the tension in my face and wait for *my ĝha* to continue.

Her eyes roam my face for a moment, and when she sees that I'm not going to react to this tiny fact, she continues.

"His name was August." She said, her voice becoming more distant. In my hearts, I know this is going in a dark direction. I can sense my *ĝha*'s grief – her anger. She confirms my fears when a tear drips down her face, "He was a good catholic man when I met him, but over time he showed his true colors. He started berating me, hurting me."

I plan to kill this husband of hers. Somehow, someway.

"One night, August was drunk," She pauses, and I can see her waver back and forth on something before she meaningfully says, "Again.

"Only this time, it escalated. Instead of beating me," Priscille's voice cracks and my hands fist at my sides, my *jisa* crackling across my skin, "He took one of the kitchen knives. Said he would kill me with it for my sins against him. It was always for *my* sins – my lust, my covetousness, my disobedience to rules he changed on a dime."

Priscille's words crack as she lets out a single sob. Her eyes drop to the floor. She cries in earnest now, her tears raining down, splattering across my rug, damning this man August with them.

I want to tell her she will never see him again, that I will take care of her, that I would *never* cause her harm, but with the earpiece in my ear, she wouldn't understand a thing, and I'm not sure I could control the rage in my voice well enough for her to understand it's not for her.

Unfortunately, her story isn't even over. She takes in a shuddering breath, and her voice is barely a whisper when she says, "I didn't know what to do, so I ran. I locked myself in our bathroom and huddled in the closet to call the *protectors of the people*. It wasn't the first time I had called them, but this time they were fast.

"I don't remember much after that; it's only snippets of the scene. August had kicked in the door and dragged me out by my hair. He had the knife to my neck, and there were officers with *weapons* trained on him. They were afraid to shoot because he was holding me against him, but he cut me and went after the officer. They shot him right in front of me.

"He died on the way to way to the *healer*."

As relieved as I am to hear that the man who my *ĝha* claimed on her home planet is dead, I know his death was too good for him. Vòllø didn't ever hurt their women, and those who did would often become overrun with so much guilt that they would end their own lives to beg forgiveness of Baso Sheva. The mere thought of laying my hands on my *ĝha* in the ways she described sickens my *jisa* on my skin. It pinches the breath in my lungs.

"I couldn't trust another man after that."

Her eyes meet mine, and I try to convey my questions. *Do you know I would never hurt you? Do you trust me, Priscille?*

Chapter Sixteen
Priscille

My fingers shake as I hold my hand out for the earbud. I'm sure Mekho has a hundred things to say, and I'm scared to hear them. My mind whirls at the possibility of his rejection, but I would understand. I may not have killed August myself – logically, I understood I was the victim – but when I was at his funeral, as the wife who wished to leave him, I was full of guilt for my choices. I felt like the sinner he said I was. So when Mekho places the device in my hand and holds it for a moment, giving me a gentle squeeze, my tear-filled eyes meet his. I'm surprised to find his stunning gray eyes clear but reassuring. When I slip my hand from his to replace the earbud, his lips tilt up at the corner.

"Priscille, I will do whatever it takes to win your trust. The way you've healed from your pain is most admirable, but you don't have to do it alone anymore. I will take it with you; I will heal it for you."

My knees buckled at his words, my blanket shield dropping to the floor. But Mekho was there to catch me. He was there to prove his words through action, and he did.

Sweeping me into his arms, his lips fell to mine gently. His kiss was like a tender caress, a way to seal his promise to earn my trust. Unexpectedly, I softened against him, feeling comforted by the powerful band of his arm around me, his firm hand tilting my chin to deepen the kiss. His tongue brushed my bottom lip, and I parted my lips slightly. I found myself eager to match the slow, comfortable rhythm he set as his tongue brushed mine.

Pressing myself against him, I feel his hardness against my stomach, and a familiar ache begins low in my core. Heat rises to my cheeks, and tentatively, I break my lips from his.

It is Abbess Carlow's voice in my mind when I meet his eyes, "When you become a nun, your life will be dedicated to God. You cannot be a nun when you are still partaking in sins of the flesh."

His eyes are so full, flushed with hazy lust, as he looks down at me, eyes darting from my eyes to my lips. The kiss was so fresh I could hardly think straight. He's still so close to me, and his delicious scent is all around me. And I'm so tempted to throw myself into the bed at my back and beg him to take me, but part of me feels like this is all so wrong. Part of me is furious at myself for going this far. The same part of me that plays Abbess Carlow's voice in my ear to keep me on the straight and narrow tells me to step away. And I listen to it.

"Are you okay, Treasure?"

I nod, still unsteady on my feet. Mekho doesn't look completely convinced, but he releases his hold on me anyway. A slight burn starts in my chest when we stop touching, and I hiss at the tiny pain, rubbing it away.

"I'm okay. Promise." I say in English, even though I know he won't understand.

His brows furrow, but he tilts his head in agreement anyway. His eyes bore into me as if he was hunting for the thoughts in my head.

A head full of lascivious thoughts. It was a great kiss, the best kiss I've ever had in my life. He executed it perfectly. From everything that came before it to the moment I ended it, Mekho got everything right. August and I never kissed like that, even when I was first falling in love with him before I ever knew who he was. No man before or after August felt like that, either. But Mekho kissed me effortlessly, and now my dirty, filthy brain that hadn't been enticed by these kinds of things in literal years wouldn't shut up.

It took physical effort to keep my body still. I'm sure I looked stiff as a board, but if I moved, I was afraid of what I would do. I was afraid of where my actions would leave me.

My mind rejected the idea that Mekho would be anything like August. His genuine promise to help me heal radiated truth like the sun's warmth on my body. But fear and guilt still shook me to my core. I had barely known him for three days, and in that time, he stole me from women I trusted, refused to tell me the truth about his cargo, and treated me almost like a pet. I understood his reasoning behind those choices, but it didn't mean I could simply trust him, no matter how much my body promised me I could. It felt disingenuous to go any further with him until I could trust my judgment.

As he takes a step toward me, I take a step back. A muscle in his jaw jumps, but he covers it with a tilt of his lips.

"May I kiss your head before I return to my duties?" He asks, holding himself still.

I nod, tilting my head in agreement as Vòllø do, and stiffen as he steps towards me. His warm lips press against my hairline, and I curse my muscles for relaxing so easily. As he leaves the room, the door clicks shut behind him. I expect to hear the solid *thunk* of the lock, but it never comes. I may not trust him, but he trusts me.

Chapter Seventeen

Mekho

Kovi catches me by surprise with her fist. My *jisa* strengthens where she hits me, but the pain still radiates across my chin. The sun set a while ago, so shadows shroud this part of the ship, giving her the perfect opportunity to smack me.

"I didn't take you as stupid, Captain," She says, grabbing me by the shirt. "Traversing the Rough Waters is one thing, especially for you to find your *ĝha*, but giving a woman, who is not even Vòllø, free reign of your entire ship? Choosing her over your *no ˇkhú* when she does not even carry her own markings?"

"Be careful what you say next, Kovilu," I warned, keeping my face neutral.

Inside, I'm burning rage. *How dare she hit me? How dare she question my bond to Priscille? How dare she question me after I worked so incredibly hard to earn my place as her captain?* On the outside, I'm unbothered. I lean against the mast beside me, crossing my arms in front of me and smirking in her direction. On the outside, I'm taunting her with my eyes, showing her I know she's just jealous.

She releases my shirt, brushing her hand across her pants. Meeting me eye-to-eye, she says, "The crew is not happy with your newest arrangements. They do not want to detour to the mainland for an *r ¨uˢad'ù* with this much special cargo beneath our feet, nor risk harming your *ĝha* while they work, nor trust a woman who doesn't even speak their language. They trust you, but trust can only go so far, and if something were to happen," Kovilu allows me to fill in the blanks.

It would be mutiny, every pirate for themselves. My crew could be forced to turn their loyalties. Loyalty I earned through years and years of proving myself to them when my mother ran the ship and in the wake of her death.

"Priscille is not a threat to our ship, and we will stash the cargo in the cove of the fiery island before we arrive at the mainland."

"And if she is injured while traipsing about the ship? She is too curious for her own good. She could go overboard on a rough wave."

Kovi always told me the truth of what I could not see, and though I did not appreciate it now, I knew she was right. I was too quick to promise Priscille complete freedom of the ship. I had been *ĝha*-blind. It seemed about more than my decisions but also the reactions of my crew. They did not trust Priscille like I did, and the only reason they had not acted on their distrust themselves was because they trusted me.

"What should I do about the crew?"

"You can do nothing. It seems you are the only one who can speak to her, and you must do it through a tiny nugget that goes in your ear. Can't you understand why the crew is nervous about this? We know nothing of her people aside from what we could get from the Valkarran captain, which was nothing."

Kovilu crosses her arms over her chest with a frustrated huff. This had obviously been weighing on her for days, but I was busy changing our route and hovering around my cabin, waiting for the moment I could be with my *ĝha* again.

"What if Priscille were to speak the Vòllø language? So she could converse with the crew, and they could get to know her? She knows a few words already. Yes and No and how to tilt her head to agree or disagree."

"It's possible it would help. If the crew could ask her some questions to learn that she is like us."

"She absolutely is. Priscille is faithful, strong – "

"She is tiny," Kovilu scoffs, holding her hand to the point on her chest where Priscille meets.

"Strong of character." I clarify, knowing my *ĝha* could face anything thrown her way – even a mutinous crew.

"And you'll speak to her about how the crew moves throughout the day so she can stay out of our way? I know what you promised her, but surely she will be amenable to a couple adjustments to keep her safe?"

"I will speak with her about it."

Kovilu turns her back to me, walking to the rail of the ship. The sun has been down, but under the light of the growing moon, we can still see the tiny crests of waves as we cut through the water. When the wind is in our sails, it feels as freeing as flight. I join her, leaning against the rail and watching the surface of the water.

"You know, the sea does not appeal the way it used to," She murmurs, scanning the many waves. "As of late, all this movement has been rough on my old bones. I'm not a maiden like Vova anymore."

I turn to look at her more closely. Kovi had been my mother's *no ˘khú*, and she should have been captain when my mother passed, but she gave it to me. She told me it was the only way I would understand my mother, and she helped me earn the respect of the crew while being hard on me herself. Now, she was telling me she was ready to leave the sea life for good. I wanted to tell her she could join me and Priscille wherever we settled, but I wasn't ready to have that conversation.

So, I asked her a question instead, "Where would you wish to settle?"

"A countryside. A small village, preferably. One where I could walk to a crystal field every morning and pray in silence, rather than praying over a tiny shard I picked up at a foreign market," She smirks. I hear my mother's voice when she says my mother's words, "Somewhere dangerous enough to feel interesting but quiet enough to find my peace."

I find the strength to ask questions I never dared to before, "Did you love her, Kovi?"

I knew my mother had no feelings for my father growing up. He was a stop on an old adventure and a person to scratch an itch. The crew had little respect for the man, but when my mom knew she was carrying his child, they all went with her to find him. He wasn't where they had met, and no one had a clue where he might have gone.

I knew Kovilu was the one to soothe my mom. She wasn't convinced she could raise me alone on the wild seas. Kovi was the one to remind her she would not be alone and that she had an entire crew to help her. And they did. Kovi was like a second mother, a much harsher one, but the rest of the crew was there, too. Every one of them taught me something about navigating the sea. Every one of them protected me before I could protect myself.

"Of course I did."

"No, I mean, did you love her the way I love Priscille?"

Kovilu smiles softly, bringing a few wrinkles to the corners of her eyes.

"Ever since I met her, I followed her everywhere. Then, she was dying, and I wanted to follow her straight to the grave, but she asked me to watch out for her son. So, here I am. Is that how much you love Priscille? Would you deny your own desires to make her happy? Even in death?"

My hearts clenched. "That's exactly how I feel."

"Then, yeah. I loved your mother more than you know, *hø*."

Chapter Eighteen
Priscille

An entire week goes by after our kiss, where Mekho barely talks to me. He came back after dark one night and told me I needed to watch out for where the sailors were working and learn some Vòllø so they could get to know me better. He told me they were a little more nervous about having me on deck than they originally let on, and then he let me sleep. Since then, he'd kept himself so busy we barely had time to talk. He came to bed late, left bed early, but never without a kiss on the forehead. Worse, this morning, he told me we had to make a tiny stop before we went to the mainland for our *r̈ uṣad'ù*, and then he immediately walked off to "make arrangements."

And now all the crew were avoiding me. Jajo catches my eyes and immediately darts away, not communicating with Ngheza and leaving her to catch sight of me and flounder as I approach.

I took Mekho's words seriously, and I'd been studying the Vòllø words by asking the crew simple questions and listening closely to their long, story-like answers. It started with me asking about what the symbols in the ledgers meant and repeating the words back to them, and then I started putting together sentence structure and doing my best to understand their meanings without my earbud. When it was Kovilu and me, I would take out my earbud completely, and she would speak slowly for me.

"Ngheza!" I call, halting her in her tracks. She and Jajo were connected at the hip most times, and they reminded me of Rihu and Royi in that they looked similar and complemented one another. Jajo was more playful and silly, while Ngheza could be more calm and serious. Both of them were obviously old enough to fit in with the *peholoe* in Wupeso; a wider spread in their *jisa* and some well-placed wrinkles told me so, but neither of them acted their age.

"Priscille," She says, grinning and bearing my sudden appearance.

"How are you?" I ask in Vòllø. This was one of the first questions I learned because I wanted the crew to know I cared about them. On Serkha's ship, many of the women had met me before I ever came aboard. The same was not true for Mekho's ship. Here, the women were kind of forced to allow me aboard, and when Mekho told me they were not as excited about that as they originally led on, I knew I needed to gain their trust.

"All is good with me, Priscille." She replies in her first language.

"That's great. That's great." I mumble, jumping to the question that truly has my attention. In Vòllø, I ask, "Can you tell me where we will dock today?"

"*Yiso.*"

"*Yiso,*" I repeat, saving the information away. "And what is in *Yiso?*"

"A safe place for the cargo," She explains. "And liquid fire. It is dangerous. You should stay in Mekho's room."

These were other words I had learned quickly. Often, the crew encouraged me to stay in Mekho's cabin, and when I wasn't busy trying to befriend them, I did. Mostly because I was hoping Mekho would eat his meals with me and check on me in there, but in the last week, he rarely did. Danger was a common word, too. They would always shout it when I was caught unaware and wandering into a place I shouldn't.

"Riṣa!" They would shout at me, and I would hop out of the way of whatever hazard I missed. I was learning quickly that I wasn't nearly self-aware enough.

"When be there?" I ask in their language, unsure of the proper grammar for the sentence I'm asking.

"We will arrive," Ngheza pauses, making sure I catch her meaning before continuing, "A sliver before sunset, I would imagine."

"You move the cargo in the dark?" I ask, my surprise coloring my words.

"Yes." She replies, nodding her head. Since I've kept her too long, Jajo comes to her rescue, sliding down a rope like Tarzan to land inches from me.

"Priscille," She greets. "I need Ngheza on the sails. And Mekho needs you in his room."

My excitement must be noticeable because they both smile in my direction as I wave goodbye to them. It wasn't a Vòllø custom to wave hello and goodbye; usually they tilted their horns to one another, reserving their waves for calling someone over. But I taught them all a few human words and customs, too, like shaking and nodding my head, waving hello and goodbye, and flipping them the middle finger. The last of which Abbess Carlow's voice reprimanded me for harshly in my mind.

But none of that mattered now because my *ĝha* wanted to see me, and I was hoping it meant we could talk for more than a few sentences because I had so many things to say.

Chapter nineteen

Mekho

Giving my *ĝha* the space she needs to thrive makes me jittery. My *jisa* has been inconsistent, no matter how many crystals I hold while I pray, and every time she enters a room, I stiffen in my pants. Yet, after My Jewel trusted me with the story of her lover on Earth, I didn't want to get physical until I had earned her trust. Now, I worried I hadn't spent enough time with her over the last week. I didn't know if she still wanted to go through with the *r̈uṣad'ù* after I sent her off to learn my language and meet my crew without being present for her.

Again, it's not that I didn't want to be around her. I only worried I would be a distraction, and now I think I was hasty in my decision.

Pacing the floor of my cabin, I don't feel like myself. I am usually calm and collected. I can't go into a drop feeling this way, like a *ĝingi* in need of a fix. But instead of *ĝingi,* it was Priscille I needed a taste of.

The door to my cabin creaks open, and I halt in place. My eyes snap to the door, and Priscille walks in wearing a dress Kovilu tailored down to size for her. It was a warm, sandy-pink color that complemented her skin and made her dark brown eyes stand out. The time on the deck had lightened streaks of My Treasure's hair, brightening her entire smiling face.

"My Jewel." Knowing she can understand my words without her earpiece makes me happy to speak with her, especially when she passes me the translator, confident in her own ability. As her hand hits mine, I wrap my fingers around hers, tugging her closer to me and placing a kiss on her forehead.

"Mekho."

I step back, putting the translator in my ear and escorting her to the desk where I have lunch set out for us. She's pleased, but her brows shoot up with surprise, and my concerns return; she thinks I've been avoiding her.

"I've missed you," I say, pulling out her chair for her. Kovi told me humans do that; apparently, it was something Priscille mentioned once when they spoke.

Thanking me, Priscille takes her seat. "If you missed me so much, why didn't you come find me?"

"I have been busy preparing for this stop, and I wanted to give you some space to get to know the crew. I'm happy I have the time for you now."

"Is this how it will always be?" She asks in her language, allowing the translator to do the work for her.

If I didn't know better, I would think Priscille wanted me around. Maybe she missed our back-and-forth earpiece conversations over dinner. Maybe she missed falling asleep with me watching over her or waking up to my face the way I missed seeing her sleepy eyes open for the day.

"Not at all," I promise. "As soon as we have completed our *r̈ uṣad'ù*, and the ship empty of cargo, we can do whatever you wish."

"And if I still wish to go to Valkarra?"

"I would beg you again to pick anywhere else." I supply easily. Her tiny eye circles roll in their sockets, and she takes her first bite of the food. It's a mix of all the things she likes most and a few new things tossed in for her to try.

Her face contorted in pleasure as the flavor of the *ifahu* fruit bursts across her tongue. Her eyes close, a soft hum emanating from her lips. The long column of her neck draws my attention as her head tilts back, leaving strands of hair to fall out of the way of the smooth skin there. Her hand is loose on her utensil, resting on the table in front of her, and I'm captivated by her as she swallows.

"Your ship has the best food."

"Our cook collected quite a variety of spices and dried goods for cooking. All the meals are things I grew up on but made better by the rewards of our travels."

She nods along, picking up words from context as she goes. She takes another bite, and I figure I ought to take one of my own, even if I do plan to watch her the whole time.

"So, *Yiso*. Everyone says I should stay on the ship, locked in here."

Her eyes meet mine, and I know she's testing me. Luckily, I knew this was coming. I'd prayed to Vova for hours before the first sliver of the sun about this exact thing. I wanted Priscille to stay on the ship, but Vova assured me she would be fine as long as she stayed at my side. Then, I spent hours trying to convince Vova of my thoughts, but the feeling inside me did not change. Priscille would touch the land on *Yiso*. According to Baso Sheva, that would be where she was most safe.

"If you stay by my side, I would be happy to have you come along," I say, taking a careful bite. Priscille studies my face, and I study hers.

"Should I stay here? Door locked? Safe and sound in bed?"

I swallow hard at the thought of my *ĝha* in my bed, waiting for me to return from a drop. Her sleeping in my shirt, the sheets all wrapped around her thick thighs... It's true, *Yiso* was dangerous, but no more dangerous than the mainland with the cargo I had stored below. If we didn't make this stop at the stash, we would be in a lot more trouble at our *r̈uṣad'ù*. And Vova had assured me she would be in more danger on the ship than by my side. As was the basic truth with all *ĝhajo*.

"I want you at my side," I vow.

She smiles, and the effect it has on my hearts is troubling. I imagine it can't be safe for them to beat like this, but I don't keel over dead.

"Then what do I need to know to survive this dangerous island full of liquid fire?"

Chapter Twenty
Priscille

We approach the blackened island at dusk. The sun is still red with the setting sun. We watch for miles as we come around the outer curve and toward the inner cove. Rising dramatically from the cool blue waters, treacherous black rock, and glowing red rivers of lava prove this island is completely inhospitable. From the peaks, smoke rises, and the smell of sulfur burns my nose. As we approach the cove, all I can see are miles of obsidian and shale and sparkling black sand beaches that look sharp and desolate.

We're moments from the turn we will take into the cove when Mekho speaks to the entire crew. Even though my Vòllø had broached the line of fluency after an entire week of constantly talking with the crew and using what I had already learned through my translation bud, he wanted me to keep the device in my ear for the mission. Which meant his words came through easily as he handed out roles and responsibilities.

It surprised no one to hear I was going to stay at his side nor that Kovilu would remain with the ship watching for mainland sailors. Jajo and Ngezha would be the main runners since they were the fastest, and we would station two people both at the cave and in the cargo bay, moving and storing the actual merchandise.

"Fast and safe," Mekho demands, eyeing each of his crew members with a shrewdness that makes me squirm.

After lunch, he left me with a gentle kiss, and I stayed in the cabin and prayed. I begged God to keep me safe with a promise that I would do his will if it became clear. Still, I mindlessly did a sign of the cross as we approached the island.

It looked like what I imagined hell to be.

Mekho dismissed the crew to get into place, and I immediately found my way to his side, standing at the rudder of the ship and watching as he guided us into the tiny cove.

"Are you ready?" He asked.

In the Vòllø language, I replied, "Ready as I'll ever be."

"Then, welcome to *Yiso*."

We come around the curve, and the ship slows immensely as we move beneath an arch of sharp black rock. Warm heat brings a thin layer of sweat to my neck once inside the cove, and I expect to see more of the same. Just above the beach, I watch a river of liquid fire run down a peak, curving away from the masses of shining black rock we approach. It would be easier to see, but in the cove, steam rises thick in the air. It's not too hot, but rather enjoyable, like a stinky steam room. And the ship cuts through it easily, like they've done it a hundred times.

I'm feeling confident as we approach the area of calm this island holds, reaching for Mekho's free hand. As his hand squeezes mine gently, I squint through the steam at something sparkling and light. It doesn't match the dark black of the terrain, and I'm confused for a moment as we slowly inch further. The sound of the water echoes around, and a red spark flies with a bang.

My neck arches back to watch the tiny red dot flare out in the sky, and I look back to where it came from. The steam thins enough for me to get a better look. Releasing Mekho's hand, I stay on the ship but approach where the spark came from.

A massive curve of silver is sunk into the sand, caressed by the black stone of the cove walls. As I inspect it, I see three massive characters carved into the side. They look suspiciously like 'SS 2.' My eyes narrow, and I try to tell myself I'm seeing things, but then another flare jumps from the top, shooting into the sky with a bang and fizzling out above me.

My mouth drops open in disbelief. It's another escape pod.

Chapter Twenty-One

Mekho

Before I can order my crew to begin, Priscille starts down the ladder Kovilu unrolled. Her feet hit the hot water before I could catch up to her, and I watched her wince, stepping into the sharp sand with wet shoes. The sharp bits attach themselves to her borrowed boots, and I force myself to move. She's running toward the fallen moon without a care for the sand monsters that curse this cove, and I'm barely hitting the sand. She's halfway to the moon when she stops, her mouth dropping open in shock.

Running forward, I meet her where she's frozen in place, wondering what about the fallen moon would make her abandon everything we discussed earlier in the day. I try not to be angry that she didn't stay by my side, but my hearts are beating double time, and I'm breathing hard from the run. I sound harsh when I speak.

"What in the name of Sheva are you doing, Treasure?"

Her eyes are wide, and her breaths are short as she stumbles forward a few more steps. The glyphs on the side of the moon become clearer as we approach, and I pull my sharpest knife from my belt, ready for danger.

I follow behind her as she runs to the moon and begins banging on its side, yelling in her human language. Some words I understand because I would never ask her to do something I wouldn't do myself, and I'd been paying attention to her words since the first time she spoke. She's calling for the moon to open and saying she's here to help. She walks around the entire thing, shouting and yelling, and when nothing happens, she pulls me toward the moon.

In Vòllø, she tells me to bang on the side of it, and I follow her directions without question, all while she pleads with the moon to open up and let her help. Her tears start, and I'm about to tell her it's a hunk of rock when a perfectly square portion of the side slides out and away in two curved slices. A long panel rolls out of the front with an unfamiliar whir.

Then, my *jisa* prickles as a small black thing aims in my direction. Two men, the same race as my *ĝha*, hold black metallic pieces in their hands that I instinctively recognize as some kind of weapon. Before I know what's happening, Priscille is standing in front of me, pleading in her language again.

"Wayt! Wayt!" She yells, trying to explain the situation. Her words tumble from her mouth faster than I've ever heard her speak, and I stay still behind her, other than to look down at her panicked face. Her arms are moving almost as fast as her mouth. One moment, she holds them out far in front of her, stopping the men from advancing. The next, she twirls them in shaking circles as she explains. I know she's talking about me because she says my name multiple times.

Mekho is good. Mekho will help. Or some long way of saying those things. Then I hear her say, 'Human' and 'Wupeso.'

I tense as she turns back to me, laying her hands on my chest. The men at the mouth of the fallen moon still have their weapons pointed in my direction, *in my ĝha's direction*, and I want to separate their heads from their bodies for the slight. Then, Priscille's tiny hands brush my markings, and I meet her eyes.

In her best Vòllø, she says, "Will you bring them to Wupeso? I know you won't go to Valkarra, but there are more humans in Wupeso anyway. They've been trapped out here for months, relying on the *escape pod.*"

I curse my voice as I growl, "Tell the men to lower their weapons."

She peeks behind herself and seems to notice the weapons for the first time since jumping in front of me. She pleads with them to lower them and makes me promise I will not hurt them, and the tension in the air settles minutely.

One man asks her a question, and her words are much slower as she explains to them. When she mentions a human named 'Roxie,' the men step out of the silver thing with surprise. I hear the word *alive* fall from one of their lips, and I can scent his relief in the air.

My *ĝha* asks a question I can't understand a single word of, and when they answer, she turns back to me. Handing me the earpiece, I know she doesn't want a single misunderstanding for the next thing she needs to say, and I place it in my ear.

Her words taint her sweet voice, "I need you to wait here while I go into the ship and speak with them. They don't trust you, and they don't want to come with us unless I can assure them. They also don't know about full-body mode for their ship's intelligence. So, I have to go put their synthetic intelligence in full-body mode."

In my limited human language, I growl, "Don't leave me. Stay at my side."

She gives me an apologetic smile. "I can't, Mekho. Trust me."

Chapter Twenty-Two
Priscille

I'm exhausted before I even step onto the pod. Mekho didn't want to let me go. The pain of watching me walk away from him was written all over his face, and the guilt in my chest for leaving the handsome pirate was almost enough to rival the guilt I felt for my inability to act like a proper nun.

As I walk up the ramp to the pod, I order Ian and Jack to leave the door open. I try to embrace my inner Roxie as I catalog the human women and children huddled together. They've been half-starved since their crash, eating some varieties of alien crabs and fish when they came close enough for the pod to catch, but otherwise, the fourteen of them were alive and well. With Jack and Ian, the ship had kept sixteen people alive.

This was the first time they had even opened the pod, according to the men, relying on the escape pod to do all the heavy lifting of defending them. But as I sat down at the data pad, I realized she was not in great shape. Being this close to the island caused a bunch of overheating errors to stack up, but the ship ignored them in favor of keeping the humans alive.

After clearing all the warnings, I speak out loud to the synthetic intelligence.

"Buttercup, can you enter full-body mode?"

"Entering full-body mode." She replies, her tone slightly rougher than Blossom's.

The huddled humans gasped as she emerged from a wall on the side of the pod in all her glory. Just like Blossom, she had all human features down to glowing green eyes. Unlike Blossom, all her decorative plating and shining metal bits were a mix of glossy greens and blacks, with soft matte green accents to give her more dimension.

Jack and Ian look shocked at the appearance of the robotic intelligence, and I try to remember whether Roxie ordered Blossom to do the same or whether Blossom had offered like she had with many of her other functions.

Handing Buttercup my earbud, I explain it's been translating the Vòllø language for me and ask if she will learn from it. She gives an affirmative, taking the tiny piece from me and pulling it apart right in front of my eyes. While I try not to grieve for the single device ensuring Mekho and I could speak and hoping she will make more, I move to the women and children.

Kneeling on the ground before them, I pick the woman toward the edge, clinging to a young child, and say, "I'm Priscille. Can you tell me your name?"

Her voice is scratchy and untested as she whispers, "Rashmi. This is my sister, Sarala."

I nod, hoping my hand is welcome as I offer it to the young girl in her lap. "It's wonderful to meet the both of you."

The younger girl gives my hand a gentle shake, though it's weak. I force myself to smile, even as my heart aches, then I continue through the others. They list off their names, and I do my best to catalog them away, introducing myself to each one and waiting until I've heard all their names to move on to my next phase.

"Here on this planet, they believe in a special goddess, Baso Sheva. And on Earth, I'm a believer in God. But even if you don't believe that I'm here because of one of them, I'm happy to have found all of you. Far away from here, there's a beautiful island where all the other humans live. It's where we were lucky enough to crash. And I'd like to bring you there."

One of the older children asks, "How?"

Heads nod in agreement all around him. I pray silently that they will still be amenable after I explain.

"Outside, there is a sailing ship with a crew full of the people of this planet. They are friendly, and the captain is a good friend of mine. You would sail with us to the village I mentioned."

"Is it safe?" One woman asks, a fearful tear dripping from her stunning steel-blue eyes.

"Much safer than this pod. Right, Buttercup?" I ask, turning to the synthetic intelligence for scientific backup.

"The odds of survival are greater with the dangerous trip across the seas than in this fried pod. Yes."

My lips thin at Buttercup's attitude, and I force myself to breathe a smile back onto my face. Blossom was always so easy to understand. A little blunt, sure, but nothing like that.

"How long will it take?"

Buttercup answers before I have the option, spouting a number I have no way to fact-check myself. "According to my calculations, the safest route will take us ten days."

"You know where Wupeso is?"

"The earbud you supplied me contains geotags with Blossom's location at creation. Obviously, I know where Wupeso is."

"Only ten more days, then I'll be somewhere safe? Sign me up." One woman says, nodding enthusiastically at the idea of leaving the pod.

"At the very least, Mekho's ship has food and fresh water," I add. "Plenty for all of us."

A chorus of growling bellies meets my ears at the mention of food, and even Jack and Ian shuffle uncomfortably behind me.

I hear one of the men's voices behind me, "Well, what do you say, crew? What do we have to lose?"

Chapter Twenty-Three
Mekho

My Treasure exits the pod several steps ahead of the small group of humans trailing after her. I'm so relieved she's okay. My body sags. Running the few steps from the bottom of the ramp to the sands in front of me, she asks in her first language, "How do you feel about sixteen extra crew members?"

A shiny green creature translates her words as Priscille speaks them, almost exactly like her tiny ear thing used to. Glancing back at my crew, I can see the nerves on their faces as the humans flood the beach, but even with the number of them, they look weak. Most of them are women like my *ĝha*, but there are also several children, and only the two men at the front of the group make me tense.

"My Jewel, have you agreed to transport these humans somewhere?"

"Duh." The green woman says, her tone sardonic, but I ignore her. I lock my eyes on my *ĝha*, waiting for her response.

"Well, yes. I was hoping maybe we could go straight to Wupeso. We could have our *r̈uṣad'ù* there. We wouldn't have to unload your cargo here. It could be their home."

My shoulders tense as I look over my shoulder at the crew, watching from the rail of the ship. Kovilu flicks her tail in my direction, a question and a warning. Then, I search the crowd of pale, thin humans. I know before I say it that I will agree to her proposition, but my words betray me, "That's a lot of decisions to have made for everyone, Priscille."

She nods, beckoning me to lean down slightly. Under her breath and in my language, she whispers, "Can you say yes now? We can talk more later?"

Her hot breath across my ear makes my *jisa* strengthen against my skin. My jaw ticks, but I tilt my horns in agreement, straightening my body and smiling at the helpless humans. Looking at the green creature, I say, "All the humans will be forced to surrender any weapons the moment they step onto my ship. Follow me."

Chapter Twenty-Four

Priscille

No one took anything from the busted escape pod except Buttercup. With a box full of spare parts, she immediately found a flat step on the ship and began creating things out of thin air and calling out the names of her pod's survivors. Soon enough, they had all returned to the huddle beside the mast with shiny new translation buds. Then, Buttercup returned with mine and an extra for Mekho. He thanked her for it, but his body was still tense from speaking with his crew.

Kovilu was furious. Even without my translation earbud, I could hear the anger in her voice. The crew had been nervous about having me on the ship, let alone sixteen more humans. We now outnumbered the crew themselves, and though there was space, she didn't like it. From what I could pick out of their conversation, they were most worried about what would happen if, on our way to Wupeso, we encountered any other ships.

Humans weren't common knowledge on Shojo yet, and the way they spoke of it made it seem that not every Vòllø would be so kind to my kind. We had no horns or tails, and Jajo said our eyes were creepy.

But Jack and Ian had given up their guns without issue, and another girl surrendered a tiny pocketknife with her name engraved on the side. We provided some basic dried rations and water to them, and the humans were so happy with their change in circumstance that they barely noticed the arguing Vòllø crew. Or if they did, they decided it didn't matter because that same crew put food in their bellies.

Luckily, the crew had come to a conclusion, and it was one they might not love, but it was the only one that would allow my plan to happen.

"Attention, humans," Mekho said, calling us all together. As much as I wanted to stand at his side, I stood with the humans as he meted out his decision, vowing that whatever he decided would affect me, too.

"My *ĝha*, Priscille, has made a promise to you that my crew and I will deliver you to Wupeso. And we will, but there are many stipulations so we can deliver you safely."

Kovilu steps in, speaking in Vòllø, though the earbuds translate for her, "One, you will stay below deck during all daylight hours. Meals will be provided, and there are plenty of bunks for sleeping, but you cannot be seen by any passing ships."

"Two," Mekho speaks again, "There will be no fighting, arguing, or otherwise raging against my crew. We are doing you a service here."

"Finally, stay out of the cargo bay," Kovilu states, narrowing her eye color in our direction. Some women gasp at the sudden change in the size of their eyes, but I'm so desensitized to it that I merely smirk.

One woman asks, "What if we have to... you know?"

"You can either wait until the sky is dark, or we will provide you with a bucket," Kovilu answers, her tone cold.

"Are you serious?" Another woman exclaims.

I eye Kovilu and Mekho and mutter, "Serious as a heart attack, I'm afraid."

"Did they keep you below deck, too?" One of the humans asks, and I shake my head.

"Locked up, yes, but not below deck. I have to be close to Mekho."

"You mean you're not going to stay below with us?" Jack asks, his chocolate brows furrowing in my direction.

I look over my shoulder to Mekho, and he speaks before I can, probably afraid I will make another decision for him after I've made so many.

"As my *ĝha*, I cannot allow her to stay below deck until she bonded to me."

"What's a *ĝha*?" Ian asks, looking between me and the protective stance Mekho has taken up one step behind me.

"A soulmate," Buttercup says. Her sarcastic commentary comes after, "How romantic."

Chapter Twenty-five
Priscille

Mekho refuses to let me escort the humans below deck. He sends Kovilu to do it instead and half-walks, half-drags me back to his cabin. I can tell he's angry with me, and I know what happens behind closed doors. I'm prepared for it to hurt as soon as we walk through the door, but Mekho isn't August.

The door shuts behind us, and his lips crash to mine. They're hot above my own, and a moan flows from my lips, reverberating against his own. My hands fly to the muscles of his shoulders as I'm pushed against the door. I have no time to think about if this is right or wrong. My thoughts of becoming a nun shatter at my feet as his tail wraps around the back of my knee, pulling it up against his hip. He grinds against my core, and I gasp against his mouth. His hands run across my body as if he's relieved it's all in one piece, and mine caresses his shoulders to assure him I'm fine.

I remind my hazy mind that he was probably more afraid of the afternoon's events than I was. All he knew was I left him to enter a strange orb that came out with more than a dozen unknown humans, some of which were armed, while he stressed alone on a beach, with a crew and illegal cargo waiting behind him. He had every right to be angry, or scared, or whatever this was.

"Never leave my side again," He growls against my ear, his lips trailing kisses and nips down the side of my neck. He pauses at my collarbone, whispering, "Never, Priscille."

My eyes find his, and I feel myself nodding in agreement. Somewhere deep inside me, I knew I wouldn't be leaving this man again. It would take God and Baso Sheva both to separate us now.

A satisfied smirk rises to his lips at my nodding, and then he kisses me again, his tongue plundering my mouth and melting me against the door in one fell swoop. One of his hands gathers my skirts, and I feel his bare hand grip my hip, tugging me even closer to him. The other hand skims across the top of my bare pussy and digs into the other hip. Then, he's lifting me as if I'm a doll full of feathers. My legs wrap around his hips, and his groan fills my mouth.

His lips are ripped from mine as my back hits the bed behind me. My skirts are up above my hips, and I try not to think too hard about my decision to give up underwear mere days after arriving on Shojo. It was so normal to walk around without them on during the day. I didn't think about what it would mean if I ever found a *ĝha*. Which I guess was a good thing. The plan was to become a nun, after all.

Sitting up on my elbows, I expect Mekho to undo the ties on his pants, but his eyes catalog my body instead as if he's trying to remember this exact moment.

"Take off the dress, Treasure."

My eyes widen slightly, but my core turns to liquid heat. In my best imitation of sexy, I loosen the ties on the dress and pull it over my head. Tossing it in his direction, I try to maintain my confidence as he groans with delight.

My body wasn't overly thin like the other girls, but I'd learned to embrace it young. The bullying remained a big part of my life, and when I didn't give up sexual favors easily, it was the first pot-shot men in bars would take, but somehow, I'd come out of it mostly okay. Yeah, the society I'd grown up in told me my body type made me less valuable. Occasionally, I admired clothes built for skinny bodies and wished maybe I was a smaller size. Still, then I would remember the dazed look of my first college boyfriend at the soft roll of my tummy or the corset my friend bought that only my boobs could fill out, and I'd fall in love with my curves once again.

Mekho didn't have to fall in love with them. He was already stunned. His eye color ate every corner of his eye, to where I couldn't tell where he looked, only that he *was looking*. Searching as if he couldn't believe I was this flawless. It brought goosebumps to my skin. His adoration was a palpable sensation in the air.

"Sheva, you're sensational."

His hands fell to my knees as he leaned over my body. Kissing me once, his lips moved down my chest, capturing my left nipple gently between his teeth. My body keened, my hand wrapping around the tip of his horn to pull his head closer. His tongue laved the small burn from his bite, tugging a small whimper from my throat. He worked his way across my chest, offering the same treatment to my other side, and his hand slid up my side, cupping my boob gently and driving me higher.

Tilting his head up, he grins in my direction. Dragging his hands up and down my sides, his thumbs graze my nipples at the top, and he watches my face contort from the pleasure.

"I promised Vova I would not take you completely until we bonded, but I never promised I wouldn't taste you." He punctuates his words with a knuckle dragged across my clit. I pinch my lips together to stop the moan, but one harsh tilt of his horns and my lips are parting again.

His eyes darken further with his lust, looking like storm clouds in the lowering light in the room. I feel him explore my pussy gently, first simply running a finger through the slickness I've created from his touch. When he brushes my clit a second time, I shiver against him, and he circles the tiny bud, watching my face intently. He finds a rhythm, making me plead for more. Pleasure skitters across my skin with each perfect touch, and I press myself toward him, begging with my eyes.

"I love it when you squirm beneath me," He rumbles, dragging his other hand from the nipple he'd been teasing to pull my thigh open further. "But I want to feel you squirm on my tongue. Can you do that for me, Treasure?"

My tongue is heavy in my mouth like I can't make it work. I try, but I fumble over the words. So, I nod and wonder if I'm drooling.

His cheeky smirk would have melted my panties had I been wearing any. Since I wasn't, it made heat pool inside me as I anticipated his tongue. I was completely unprepared for what he had planned.

In one quick move, his arms barred around my thighs, dragging my slick pussy up to his mouth, leaving only my shoulders resting on the bed. With his tongue flat, he licked from my center to my clit, latching onto the bundle of nerves there and sucking.

His rumble of pleasure buzzed against my clit as his tongue worked a new combination, making me whimper and pant beneath him. He didn't seem to mind when my thighs tightened around his head or when I came crashing over the edge. He simply lapped at me faster, groaning at the taste and whispering a bunch of sweet nothings I could not hear from his muffled position. But he also didn't stop. Slowing himself slightly, he moved away from my sensitive clit to taste my center more.

Keeping himself between my legs, he gently lowered my hips to the bed before finally glancing up at me from between my shaking thighs.

"I want you to come again, but this time, on top."

Chapter twenty-six
Mekho

The sweet honey between Priscille's hips is the real treasure of a *ĝha*. Nothing would ever be as sweet on the tongue as her pussy while her thighs clenched around me. It was a genuine treat, and I needed it day and night. I needed to hear her soft cries of pleasure, feel her hands tighten around my horns, probably a dozen more times between now and our arrival in Wupeso. At least a dozen more times, I resolve, tilting my horns.

Her hazy eyes dart from my face, covered in her juices, to the breadth of my chest. She bites her lip gently, and it pulls a smirk to my lips. My *ĝha* likes my body as much as I like hers. Yanking off my shirt, I toss it away toward her dress and crawl onto the bed, dropping a knee between the heat of her thighs.

Pushing herself onto her elbows, her lips capture mine, and it sends the heat straight to my groin. The flavor on her tongue and her heat on my lips is a pure aphrodisiac, and I hate Vova at that moment because I wish to plunge my rock-hard cock inside my sweet Priscille. I wish to watch her eyes roll back, her lashes flutter as her hot pussy clenches around me. I wish to feel her spasm of pleasure pulse all around me while she sees the love I have for her in my eyes.

Instead, I lie back against my pillow and direct her to straddle my face. She crawls towards me on her hands and knees, and my stomach tenses with anticipation. Her hand brushes over the stays of my pants, my eyes squeeze shut, and a noise of pleasure escapes me. Her tiny, soft hand brushes up the center of my stomach, and I force my eyes open to look at her. Priscille's dazed smile brings a smirk to my face.

I catch her wrist, tugging her against my chest and off balance. Her bare skin presses against my own, and my *ĝha* marks flash. My free hand pulls her face to mine, and she meets my kiss with fervor. When she breaks it, her eyes meet mine, and I give her a genuine smile.

"Enough playing now, Priscille. Let me taste you again."

I offer her my hand for stability as she slings her thigh over my face. Guiding that same hand to my horn, I feel her grip on me. My tongue reaches up, flicking the tiny bundle of pleasure at the apex of her thighs, and I hear her muffled moan.

She tentatively grinds down on my face, and my hands find the tops of her thighs, spreading her wider and pulling her closer, tonguing her hot pussy at the same time. Her gasp of pleasure makes my cock strain against the stays of my pants, but I focus on the beautiful being above me.

Sliding my tongue lower, I dip it into the source of her honey, dragging it in and out until I'm fucking her with my tongue. Dragging one hand up her thigh, I use my thumb to rub circles over her clit, matching the rhythm of my thrusts. Soon enough, she's grinding down onto me, calling my name as I lick and suck her with my mouth.

She moans my name above me, "Mekho, yes. Oh, Oh. I'm so close."

Doubling down my efforts, I lick and thrust with my tongue while my fingers work her clit. My own groans of pleasure seem to push her higher, and with my free hand, I glide up her body to tease her responsive nipples, but she catches her hand with my own, wrapping it tighter around her mound as she grinds on my face, drenching me with her juices.

A muffled knock comes at the door right as I'm about to pull her over the edge, but we both ignore it. Her thighs clench, and I can hear her soft voice above me as I work to wring pleasure from her body beneath her. "Oh. Oh. Wait. Oh. *Yes.*"

A fresh burst of her flavor explodes across my tongue, and I move my fingers, lapping at her honey as if it's my last meal. I'm still going when she squeaks, throwing herself off my face and snatching the small blanket to wrap herself in. She dives off the edge of the bed, her eyes peeking at the door, and I come up on my elbows as it creaks open.

Two of my crew members are hiding there in the shadows, looking away from the bed as they spew apologies.

"Sorry. So, sorry, Captain."

"We heard a yes, we thought –

"It doesn't matter what we thought, we – I'm sorry, Lady Priscille. Captain. It's just, we, um, we needed some direction on the course. You said you would meet us before dusk."

Looking straight at Priscille, I lick my lips with a smirk.

"No problem. I'll meet you on deck right after I finish up here."

They mumble a few more apologies before shutting the door, but I don't look their way once. My eyes are stuck on Priscille. As she throws my shirt at me from the floor, pure satisfaction drips through me. Her pink cheeks tell me everything I need to know.

Chapter Twenty-seven
Priscille

God is punishing me. He must be. Why else would I finally accept that maybe, just maybe, Mekho was my soulmate, fated to be with me across space and time, all so we could get interrupted by crew members I will never look in the eye again? *Where is Clara when I need her? Damn it.*

Dressing in one of Mekho's clean shirts, I pad across the room to the tiny prayer altar he has and kneel to pray. I beg for forgiveness, only feeling worse as my words drag on. As if my intuition finally kicked in, my guilt arises when I apologize for the acts we did. My guilt comes from apologizing for something I know Mekho believed was sacred. The words felt like some kind of betrayal to him, and that made my skin crawl.

With a sigh, I roll from my knees to my butt and lean back on my hands. Outside the windows, stars sparkle in the sky, the only deviation from the dark sea below us. I'm silent, but I finally see it. The reflection of the moonlight on the water carves into the waves. Inside that canvas of darkness and light, I could almost see a youthful face and long, sparkling hair.

Wanting a closer look, I scramble to the window, but the face does not disappear. The surface seems like a living, breathing entity. So, I close my eyes and listen to the waves. An undulating melody of boundless sound seems to echo inside me, only disturbed by the methodical direction of the ship through the waters. Then, I can smell the salty sea air all around me and taste it on my lips. With my eyes open, I step toward the window, resting my hand against the cool glass and watching in wonder.

I could see Baso Sheva in the waves, I could feel her in the coolness of the glass, and I suddenly understood exactly what Serkha told me about. My heart knew the truth of their deity, and it didn't invalidate the beliefs I held of mine. It only strengthened them.

If there was physical evidence of The Baso Sheva in the ocean, in the mate marks, in the *jisa,* I could reasonably believe there was physical evidence of my own God in the blessing it was to land here. To find myself on a planet with a livable atmosphere, friendly people, and enough technology to make the transition comfortable it had been God the whole time. Putting me here, with Mekho, had to have been God too. Right?

Chapter Twenty-eight
Mekho

After three sun cycles of being cooped up, the humans become antsy. They know it will take ten days, but being in such cramped quarters, knowing the end is in sight, had driven them a little mad. Jack and Ian, the two human men, came to blows this morning, and Kovilu had to break them up. One child tried to sneak into the cargo bay to look for a toy, and Lakhu scared the poor creature into peeing their pants. The adult woman in charge of that child was furious with Lakhu and demanded to see the captain.

Now, I was standing in the bunks, realizing how bad it was. Though we said they couldn't come out during the day, none of them had bothered to try a little walk at night, sleeping away the hours easily. Unfortunately, it meant their minds began to shatter.

Two children sat across from one another, smacking their hands together and singing under their breath, and they were the least concerning set of humans I laid eyes on. One of the adult women, Priscille had introduced her as Rashmi, was sitting up on a bunk, rocking on her toes as if it were the most interesting thing in the world. The poor woman's hair was dull, and she had not fully recovered from the state of semi-starvation they experienced in their pod. In fact, none of them had fully recovered. Another woman was sick, bent over the bucket with an unnatural green hue to her skin. Some humans slept, and most of the children played, but the morale was low. So low it crept along my *jisa,* draining my energy.

"There will be dinner on deck after dark," I announce. It was Priscille's plan. When I explained all my crew's concerns to her, she said they needed to "stretch their sea legs." She suggested dinner on the deck and some kind of game. She said she needed to get out, too. Being inside my spacious room still felt like a prison.

Rashmi's head snapped up as if she hadn't even realized I was there. Buttercup, the metallic green woman, had provided all the humans and me a translation bud. So, I knew Rashmi understood my words, yet she looked angry.

My eyes narrowed in her direction, and I smirked. It was a challenge to see if she had something to say. Her fists clenched the edge of the bunk, and she looked away again, watching her feet.

Satisfied with the humans' response, I turned to leave the bunks. My crew would be the next to hear the news, and I needed to warn them to be on their best behavior. Over the past three days, they had felt cramped in their bunks, complaining of the children's crying – and the women's. Their already poor opinion of humans was growing poorer with each passing day.

Priscille assured me they only needed to get to know them individually – that the humans and the crew could grow to like one another if they weren't constantly crammed together and half-starved.

I was only a couple steps from the exit when a child tugged on my pant leg, pulling my attention down to them. Peering up at me with their distinctly human eyes, the child asked, "What's your name?"

Not wanting to scare the tiny thing, I take a knee.

"I'm Mekho."

"Are you the Captain?"

"I am."

"My mama says you're an alien. Is that a bad thing?"

I chuckled. Turns out children were the same no matter what planet you came from. Endlessly curious creatures with no sense of self-preservation, they asked plenty of questions and got into plenty of trouble.

"You are the alien on my planet, but that's not a bad thing. In fact, without you, my kind may never have survived."

"Without me?" The child's eyes seemed to light up with excitement. "So, I saved you?"

More or less. "You sure did."

"I'm like a superhero?" The child doesn't wait for an answer, spinning off to run toward their friends, saying, "Guys, we're superheroes! We saved the world."

Straightening from my crouch on the floor, I watch the child for a moment more before turning to leave. A soft voice from the shadow whispers, "Thank you for doing that. That will carry Carter all the way home."

"But I'm hungry now," Niti complains. She was the first to speak after the announcement. We sat in silence while they allowed Kovilu to glare at me. I didn't cave to her attitude, but I respected her, so it was no easy feat. Unfortunately, Niti's words set off an entire symphony of complaints.

"Why do we have to wait for the humans?"

"Because we need to improve the relationship between the crew and the humans," I explain.

"Why? We're only with them for a few more sun cycles."

This was another thing Priscille, and I had discussed. After we landed in Wupeso, Priscille and I would host our *r̈ u̥ṣad'ù*, and she wanted to stay. I hoped the crew would learn to like humans and want to stay, too. I already knew Kovilu was on board. When Priscille explained Wupeso's land to her, Kovi smiled for the first time since my mother died. Unfortunately, I didn't want to have that conversation yet.

"I need you to befriend them to make the travels easier. It will please Priscille."

A round of grumbles went out among my crew, and I realized then they were less behaved than the children below deck. Yet, they learned to love my *ĝha*. Before we had translation buds, she had learned enough to have authentic conversations with each of them. Slowly, she won them each over.

Though Kovilu acted otherwise, she was the quickest to love my *ĝha*. Which was now obvious in the way she took Priscille's side of the argument in almost everything. When I tried to convince Priscille it would be best to go to the mainland first, Kovilu stood behind Priscille with crossed arms as Priscille argued for Wupeso.

Then, it was Jajo and Ngheza. Since Baso Sheva herself connected them, they fell together. Priscille won them over with the gruesome tales of the ship that brought her here. After she explained space travel vessels to them and guns, they were her new best friends.

The last powerhouse she had to topple was Niti, and the rest of the crew would follow, but she had yet to find her soft spot. The crew was divided because of it.

"If it's for Priscille, why didn't she ask?" One of my sailors asks.

"She's human," Kovi responds as if the sailor is slow of mind.

They bicker between one another some more, and the ship grows louder with it. When Lle stands, I know I have to step in again.

"Enough!" I shout, "You will all wait to eat dinner like the humans must. You will all attend dinner like my *ĝha* requests. And you will all behave until dismissed."

They all shut up, staring in my direction. Their silence allows the sound of the waves lapping against the boat to echo around us. It's silent otherwise, and Jajo raises her tail.

"Yes, Jajo?" I ask, exasperation coloring my tone.

"Are we dismissed, Captain?"

My eyes scan my crew once more. All these incredible women have trusted me for so long, and now...

"Yeah. Dismissed."

The grumbles of my crew will echo in my ears for hours to come.

Chapter Twenty-nine
Priscille

Buttercup is like the grouchy teenage version of Blossom. This becomes apparent when I ask her to test the rest of the pod survivors for allergies and compare it against the foods the cook prepared for dinner. Not only did she grumble about the task, but then she complained the entire time she did it. I didn't even know synthetic intelligence could complain. Blossom certainly never did.

Luckily, everything prepared for the night was edible for the humans on board except one tiny fruit that Jack was allergic to.

Since Buttercup wasn't human, she had assumed the rules didn't apply to her, and she traversed the deck as she pleased. This was both a positive and a negative. It made her a great go-between for me and the rest of the humans, and since she could communicate with the crew, she could stay out of everyone's way. That was something I was still perfecting.

As the sky darkened above me, I finished slipping into one of my two dresses. The one created for me. In Wupeso, the women donated tons of their old clothing to the humans and helped tailor it to us. Then, after Vera and Kano were married, they taught us to make our own with the fabrics we picked.

The one I arrived on this ship with was a dress I'd sewn myself.

Some of the Vòllø thought it was overly modest, but since I'd been trying to be a nun, I felt it was perfect. Long, cream-colored sleeves reached my wrists, and I gave it a mock neck. A bib-necked dress in a berry pink color went right over the top. In Valkarra, I had a little makeup and a lip color that matched the dress perfectly, but here, I did my best to braid back my hair.

For a moment, I felt a little guilty because I knew the other humans aboard were wearing spare clothes from anyone on the crew who could spare them, and they'd been difficult to roll and pin in a way that made them wearable. But those spare outfits allowed them to wash their clothes at least enough to wear them again.

Before I leave the room, I kneel at the altar and say a prayer. With a sign of the cross, I exited Mekho's room to join the crew and humans on the deck.

Aside from dinner, I had a plan for tonight. The humans felt cooped up, frustrated, and tired. The crew was grouchy, cramped, and distrustful. They all needed to let a little bit go, and there was one thing I knew would work like a charm.

Church ball.

Or rather, team sports of any kind.

Many of the nuns I met during my discernment period played or supported the parishes during church sports games. It was one activity I didn't want to leave behind when I became a nun, and it surprised me to find many non-cloistered sisters who enjoyed watching and playing sports in the same way.

The games always had everyone feeling a little bit happier going through the week, and even Abbess Carlow said a relaxing activity like that was Godly. Which is why I figured it couldn't hurt.

But first, we had to make it through dinner.

Most of the crew had already gathered around the table. Mekho explained they were extremely grumpy to put off their normal eating time, but after he pulled the captain card, they begrudgingly agreed to attend. However, the humans were still arriving. With all the tiny kids below, I wasn't surprised the humans didn't arrive together or in any organized pattern. Jack was the first to arrive, and he said the rest of the humans would join soon – Ian was helping below. Then Rashmi and her sister came, and a few of the other women followed behind, but Ian still hadn't come out, nor the kid Carter that Mekho met earlier.

When I was certain we were about to inspire mutiny, they finally joined us. The woman in charge of Carter was apologizing profusely, which neither Mekho nor myself listened to. Dinner was finally served, and I was determined to start a few friendly conversations and bring everyone closer.

Since we were all eating together, we sat on the floor of the deck, listening to waves and eating under the illumination of glowing lamps. Funky patterns of light wove over the sun-warmed wood, and the sound of wooden plates and utensils scraping against dishes filled the air. The humans seemed to watch what I'd taken and follow my lead because many of their plates seemed identical.

Some kids were adventurous about what they tried, encouraged by the Vòllø women eating like they were the ones half-starved instead. While other children only tried things that looked familiar to them – like the *llige* and the tiny quarters of fruit that tasted like vanilla coffee creamer and cherries combined. Aside from Jack, it seemed like all the adults tried a little of everything, picking and choosing their favorites.

I don't realize my knee is bouncing until Mekho's hand falls to it, keeping it still beneath his steady grip. When I look up at him, he's smirking in my direction. My own excitement to be on the deck fuels me, and though I wasn't big on hiking or running, I loved a good sports game. Especially something like the one I had planned that would require some teamwork.

A few conversations spark up between the crew and some of the more outgoing humans, but otherwise, dinner is mostly bowl scraping and extra servings. Until it's finally time for the main event.

As people are wrapping up their dinner, Mekho and I stand. Before the Death of Baso Sheva, they had apparently played a game called *b'iva*. The idea of the game was to get a ball into the basket atop the main mast before the other team could, but some rules required everyone to work together as a team.

First, the ball can never be off the deck unless it's in someone's hand. So, throwing the ball – not allowed, passing it hand over hand – all good. Kicking the ball was also totally fine.

Second, before going to the goals, players have to get the ball to an ownership zone first, which is the deck above the captain's quarters, where the rudder is located. As soon as the ball hit the top of the steps, it would be owned by the team that got there first.

Finally, once you own the ball, it can be brought to the nest above the mast by any means necessary. Climbing would be best, but you can throw it if you're willing to take the risk of missing and breaking team ownership of the ball.

Since Mekho and I discussed this the night before, we would be team captains, and our first round would be teams of both humans and Vòllø. Then, if it went well, we would play a human versus Vòllø game for funsies – and earn a little respect from the crew.

So, Mekho explained the rules, and I picked the first teammate. Looking right at my *ĝha,* I announce, "My first pick is Carter."

"Yes!" A little girl screeches, tearing away from her mother to stand beside me. She couldn't be over four years old, and she stood mid-thigh on me, but she was a superhero, so I had to have her on my team.

"Kovi," Mekho announces as if I didn't see that coming from a mile away.

Bending down to Carter's level, I ask her who we should pick next, and we end up with her mom on our team. Mekho picks Jack from the human side, then I pick Niti. So far, Niti and I haven't been the best of friends, but I'm hoping this game will change things. On and on we go until we are even teams of twelve players each. Buttercup will be the one to drop the ball. Then, we get a few minutes to talk strategy.

The Vòllø on my team are quick to throw out their ideas, having played the game before.

Jajo is the first to speak, "Mekho will make Ngheza his climber because she's fast but not faster than me."

"Makes sense," I agree, "So Jajo climbs the mast, but first, we have to get it into the own zone."

"As team captain, wait in the own zone where you can see the field," Niti explains, her own excitement for the game overriding her dislike of me. "That way, you can direct us further."

"Does that sound agreeable team?" I look directly at the kids when I ask.

Carter nods, and the two other children on our team follow her lead. Looking to the adults, I ask what else we need to strategize. The fiery Italian woman, who has been conversational since she found out she was being saved, says, "I will defend from the other team."

"You? You're tiny." Niti said, pulling a glare from the five-foot Italian. I keep my smile to myself, knowing exactly how proud that 'tiny' woman is. Fiamma glares Niti down until the Vòllø caves. "Fine, you win. Defend at your own risk, but Lakhu should be your extra teammate there."

I look at Lakhu, and she nods her agreement. The woman was built like a linebacker, so I had to agree with the sentiment. Standing beside Fiamma, their difference in size was comical.

Before I can continue, Niti says, "Everyone else, you're runners. You run where Priscille tells you to run, and you pass the ball. *Never* let it stay in the air. Kovi will catch it, and we won't see it again. If you're not close enough to hand it off, kick it or roll it, but do not throw it."

"Kick it or roll it, but do not throw it," The children repeat robotically.

I look up from my huddle to see Mekho is already standing around with his team. I must admit they look prepared. Even though he ended up with two more kids on his team than I did and fewer Vòllø overall, he seemed to get the strongest players of both teams. He had both the human men, Kovilu, and two massive deckhands.

When he catches my eyes, his smirk grows, and I narrow my eyes. His *jisa* crackles brightly, and I shoot him a wink, hoping it will throw him off. But he does one better; running a hand under the hem of his shirt, I get a glimpse of his solid body, and my mouth goes dry. I know I must win this. Everyone moves into position. The ball drops. Game on.

Chapter Thirty

Mekho

Our team's name is 'The Winners.' It was Jack's idea to come up with one, and the other humans on my team loved spitting out their ideas. We considered being the pirates, but I knew my Priscille would tease me until the day I died for that one, so I waited for more to come through. Then, the tiny boy Myles suggested 'The Winners.' The Vòllø on our team loved it, especially Kovilu, who clapped the child on the back as if he were her own.

Now, Jack stood in the own zone with my *ĝha*, calling out the shots as we moved around the deck. Currently, Priscille's team had the ball, but I was defending the stairs, so I couldn't wait to see them try and get around me.

"Hand it off to Carter," I hear Priscille direct, watching Jajo pass the ball to the superhero I met below deck. Carter takes the ball, rushing at me as if she can take me on herself. She's a tough little thing, but she can't think she could get past me. Right?

She darts to my right, and I reach out my arms to snatch the ball from her, but she slips beneath my legs and scrambles up the stairs behind me. From the top of the steps, she hands the ball to Priscille before saying, "Mekho, watch this."

I reach for her again, but I miss her completely as she dashes across the own zone to the side her team is defending. They chose a tiny woman for the job, with Lakhu as a backup, and it wasn't the strategy I would have chosen for myself. I can't do anything but watch as Lakhu passes Carter through the air into Jajo's waiting arms.

They never threw the ball itself, but the person holding it. It was a brilliant idea.

It didn't take long after that for Jajo to scale the mast and toss the ball into the waiting net. Priscille was easily the loudest. Stomping her feet on the deck, clapping her hands, and whistling, she celebrated as her team surrounded her. Dancing together in a circle, they chanted, "Kick it, or roll it! Whatever you do, don't throw it! Goooo Pirates."

Chapter Thirty-one
Priscille

High on my win, I was stoked as the humans gathered around. Together, my team and I had shown the entire crew what human ingenuity looked like. Carter was a fearless little girl, willing to sail through the air and face a Vòllø man head-on, but she wasn't our only strength. Watching the other humans during our first round pointed out a lot of things we could use to our advantage.

Jack was a skilled tactician. The original set-up their team discussed was obviously his idea from the way he ordered their pieces around the board. He knew exactly where to put each player for the best return, yet he didn't know about our secret weapons. So, with that in mind, I offered him the own zone.

The kids all had an advantage because the Vòllø were afraid to hurt them. More fragile than their Vòllø counterparts, human children didn't have horns or *jisa* to keep them defended, so the Vòllø didn't like to get physical with them and often stuck to reaching for them and trying to pick them from the ground. Since they were so close to the ground, that was an advantage too.

Then, we had Rashmi and Victoria. Secret rogues, those two. Every time I looked around the deck, they were in different places, and they were *always* open for a pass.

Ultimately, we decided Ian and Fiamma would defend together. The kids would keep the ball moving where the Vòllø couldn't reach it, Rashmi and Victoria would get it to Jack so it was owned, and I would climb the mast. Was I qualified to climb the mast? No. Did I want to? Also, no. But did I want my team to win? Yes. The mast had tiny rungs to make climbing easier, and I was determined to win. Plus, once I was above halfway, it was a win anyway. No one could defend past there.

"Are we ready team?"

"Almost. We need a name."

"How about the superheroes?" I offer.

Carter beams, and the kids nod with enthusiasm. Ian claps his hands together. "Alright, superheroes. Let's win this thing."

Being on deck is an entirely original experience. The energy is rougher, and the competition feels fiercer, but I don't let it get to me. God is on my side. The first round was all about learning the game, but this is where it really mattered. Human versus Vòllø was about earning the respect of the crew, and we were sure we could do it. Like in our first game, we planned several contingencies for when things went sideways – a perk to having two ex-military on our team and a whole bunch of creative kids.

It started off like the last game. They dropped the ball from the top of the nest, and everyone immediately dove for it. The kids wait until the victor emerges and then *swipe*. Myles snatched the ball straight from Ngheza's fingertips as she tried to pass it to Jajo, passing it off to Theo, who kicked it to Carter. Carter snatched it beneath her arm, looking for an opening, but she couldn't find one.

"Victoria! Left," Jack called from the own zone. Carter looked both ways, and I realized she probably wasn't confident in her right and left yet. Unfortunately, Kovilu snatched the ball from her as she tried to figure it out.

Jack's patience impressed me as Carter tried to get her head back in the game. He called, "Good job, Carter. You'll get it next time."

Still, Kovilu runs past our defense, planning to pass the ball to the defense on her own set of steps. The steps I was waiting at the bottom of for our plan. Kovi passes off the ball, and Niti passes it up the steps without looking. Jack snatches the ball from Niti with a grin and slides onto his belly to pass it into my outstretched hands.

I don't hold onto it. Passing it immediately back to Carter, who dashes between legs, kicking it away as she needs to. Instead of paying too much attention to the back and forth of the ball, I find my way to the bottom of the mast and up the first few rungs. Rashmi gets the ball from Myles and makes it to the ladder to pass it to me.

Adrenaline pumps through my veins as the humans cheer, and I stick the ball between my shirt and dress. Climbing as fast as I can, I hear Jack shout, "Faster, Pris." Huffing a breath, I try to improve my speed, but I can hear the Vòllø cheering beneath me, and I make the ridiculous choice to look down.

Mekho climbs two rungs behind and gaining. I squeak, using one hand to shove the ball tighter into my shirt and doubling down on the power. Now that I know he's right there, I can feel him like a shock of electricity. Every time his hand hits a rung, it's like a warning that my feet need to be hitting another one. I'm almost to the halfway mark when I feel his hand land on my foot, and I kick my sandal into his face as I jump.

Looking to the top, I climb like the wind, ripping and roaring up the rails as fast as Jajo did. When I look back, Mekho is stuck at the halfway mark, holding my shoe with a smirk.

I make it to the top, drop the ball into the nest, and hold my arms out wide as the humans cheer with victory once again.

Once our victory is announced, Mekho climbs the last jaunt of the tower. Kneeling before me, he slips my sandal back on my foot, then surging forward, he kisses me in front of everyone.

They all cheer, but the only thing I can hear is the steady thump of his two hearts beneath my palms.

Chapter Thirty-Two
Priscille

The game is such a success the entire group eats together every night before picking teams for another round. Not everyone plays, but now we have a small group of referees and cheerleaders each night. Usually, Jane, Ian, and the gunners on the crew. They usually settle close touches or point out when a ball moves in the air, but mostly, they cheer for both teams when they're succeeding. It goes this way for another two nights.

Tonight, we're playing the first game with Mekho and me on the same team. I've sent him up the mast when he shouts, "Stop! Hide!"

He's halfway to the top of the nest as the Vòllø panic, directing humans into the captain's cabin or to lie down on deck beneath musty tarps. Dragging the children into my room with me, I close the door tight, directing everyone into dark nooks and crannies hidden from the window. I hear Kovilu lock the door behind us. Then, I find my way to the prayer altar and press myself against the wall beneath the window.

We're all silent as the ship cuts through the water. I make the sign of the cross and pray silently. Ten minutes pass, then twenty, then thirty.

The lock unlatches on the cabin, and Mekho steps in, his face grim.

"All clear." He says to the humans, but no one is in the mood to keep playing. They all shuffle out quietly, yawning and heading toward the steps to the bunks. I don't stand until they're all gone.

"Was it other pirates? The Valkarrans?"

He shakes his head, obviously distraught by the passing ship in the night, but he doesn't say more until I take his hands.

"Mainlanders, but it's odd. They never come this far."

"Do you think they found the pod? That they're looking for us?"

"They wouldn't even know what you were. I haven't taken you there. And when I did, you would have stuck close, worn a hood. We would have stayed out of sight and out of trouble."

"You were going to smuggle me into sacred lands?"

He shakes his head and pulls me close. For whatever reason, the mainlanders had him shaken, and that was not something I wanted to hear. As far as I knew, Mekho was the fiercest pirate in the entirety of Shojo. If he thought a mainland ship was bad news, I didn't want to find out for myself.

Chapter Thirty-Three
Mekho

I watched Priscille's chest rise and fall, hoping it could soothe my anxious hearts, but I couldn't stop thinking about what the mainlanders were looking for. Valkarrans would have been a welcome sight comparatively, but we were not so lucky. The mainland ship passed with a friendly wave, and Kovilu navigated us past without issue, but we were approaching the Rough Waters, and little else went this way.

These were the fears that fueled my dreams when I finally fell asleep. Nightmares plagued me. The mainland ship coming back this way, stealing the humans my crew now loved, driving past the Rough Waters on our tail and finding Wupeso – a village completely under-prepared for the war the mainland would rage. The fear that I was bringing danger and shame to a gentle city invaded my mind, and I thrashed in my sleep like the waves outside my windows.

When I finally woke, Priscille was still asleep, and rain poured outside. The sea was an angry, whirling mess of choppy waves and thundering clouds. It was a terrible omen for our travel across the Rough Waters.

Finding my way onto the deck, my crew was working hard. With the sails secured, Kovilu maintained the rudder against the harsh gusts of wind and sea spray. Deckhands tied down goods, securing things to the mast as needed and shoring up any slats below that may have been in ill repair.

"We should ride out the storm before attempting to cross the Rough Waters," I shout to Kovilu.

"That could take many cycles and push us farther off course." She responds. "With the humans aboard, we have a full crew. We should use them and do our best to reach Wupeso."

I consider my *no ˇkhú's* words carefully. Kovi was right about the storm throwing us further off course. Kovilu could battle with the rudder for a time, but the harder she fought, the more likely it would be to break. At some point, she would have to release it and let the waves take us where they may. If we navigated the Rough Waters in this storm, the happenings in the depths could pull the ship under and swallow us whole. Or Baso Sheva could guide our way, delivering us safely from storm and sea.

The icy rain pelts my *jisa,* dripping down my skin and soaking through my clothes. They suction to my body, sticking to my skin and making me look like the sea itself. Watery and raging.

After the scare from the mainlanders, I wanted to be across the Rough Waters as fast as possible. I couldn't risk our ship washing up against the back of their islands and setting us back days. As it was, the humans craved the sunshine. Priscille would stare longingly out of my special windows, wishing she could feel it on her skin. The humans below would talk about our games and say it would be better if they had the light of the sun on their side – not that they needed it to win.

The sky growled, the rain picking up further with my hesitance. Then, sharp lights crackled across the sky in a bright red streak.

As if I summoned her with my thoughts, Priscille emerges from my cabin in the dress she arrived in. She doesn't seem to mind the chilly rain as it drenches her clothes, streaming down her hair and into her eyes. She hustles to my side and tucks herself beneath my arm.

"We have to get out of the storm. What is your plan?" She shouts. Another rumble of thunder cracks through the sky, punctuated by angry streaks of red light, temporarily casting an angry hue.

"Kovilu says we should cross the Rough Waters."

"It gets rougher than this?" She asks, looking up at the sky. A hint of fear pulls at the corners of her mouth, and I run a soothing hand across her side.

"We would need everyone but the children to work together to make it."

"Have you asked them?" She asks, brushing away the water streaking across her face.

"Not yet."

Her hand clasps mine tightly, and she marches with purpose to the bunk entrance. Climbing below deck, we find all the humans awake and huddled together like they were in the pod. Jack and Ian seem to stand guard, watching the sides of the ships warily as if they don't trust the craftsmanship.

"Sounds pretty bad out there." Ian offers. One child, Myles, I think, clings to his leg.

Priscille is way ahead of me. Crouching before the children, she asks them to be brave, to rely on one another, to be superheroes. It doesn't take long for me to realize she's preparing them for the loss of adults. They would all be coming above, learning to help navigate a ship through a storm.

"We're going to need help to get the ship out of this mess. It was unexpected, but we have enough hands if you are willing."

I watch their bravery come over them. Steeling themselves against death at sea, they all stand together, releasing the children to stay below deck. Carter, the brave girl she is, wishes to join, but Priscille convinces her to stay behind and keep the children safe. She runs the point through by saying it's what a superhero would do. The adults with siblings and children give them hugs and kisses and warn them to stay down here until they come back. Then, we are all stepping into the rain and preparing for the battle to come.

Chapter Thirty-four

Mekho

According to my mother, my father was a warrior. He fought on land, blessed by the moon. She told me I was a warrior too, but I fought at sea, blessed by the waters so they could never defeat me. She told me I was a part of this landscape, and even if it ever took me from my ship, I would not feel fear because I belonged to it. But I didn't belong to the sea anymore. I belonged to a small human woman with deliciously wide hips and a faithful soul.

I wondered if that was why Baso Sheva was angry with me, why it would give me this obstacle before I could bond with my *ĝha*. But Priscille assured me we would make it through the storm and across the Rough Waters. She assured me in both her God's name and mine.

Pairing off the humans with each Vòllø was a feat, and many of my crew did not want them above deck, even though they knew they were useless below. Kovilu helped me direct the people, and we tied each of them at the waist to the mast.

I was standing before my *ĝha* as the rain assaulted us, shielding her with my back as best I could. A thick rope created heat between my fingers as I dragged it around her thick hips, securing it on her waist. I talked her through the knot and warned her not to undo it for any reason. She agreed to my terms and joined Niti. Everyone had to work together for this to work.

With everyone secured, I met Kovilu at the top of the ship and helped her pull the rudder into place. Jajo and Ngheza dropped a sail, using their entire bodyweight to tug it into place, and then we launched ourselves into the storm.

Time seemed to speed up, and chaos reigned. The ship was tossed side to side, and we crested waves so large I was sure they would pull us beneath. But the ship stayed upright. The waves crashed around us, never tilting us too far. I wanted to keep my eyes on my *ĝha*, but I trusted Niti's capable hands, and I focused on directing us past the worst of the storm.

I narrowed my eyes into the choppy sea, searching for loose debris or waves that would pull us all under, and helping Kovilu navigate accordingly. Others below moved ballasts, keeping us stable through the storm, or they helped reduce the sail to control our speed. My crew was a well-oiled machine beneath me as we fought against the angry sea.

Yet, it did not stop coming. The rain poured down in icy sheets, railing against my *jisa* with a stinging force. Thunder and lightning crackled and boomed above us, striking out as if it wished to turn my ship to ash on the water. Waves jerked us left and right for hours. Kovilu and I switched out duties, letting me steer the rudder as she looked on and navigated us through. My shoulders were burning from the efforts, but I trusted her innately.

When I could barely hold the rudder, she would switch me, and on and on, it went. Then suddenly, the storm waned.

The clouds thinned before us, the thunder ended. Lightning stopped raging against the sky, seeking to hit my ship with its fire. The waters soothed to their usual blue waves instead of the dark and shady masses they were moments ago. The rudder moved with ease through the water, and within a sliver of the sun — we could see it. Real sunlight on the water. It sparkled and warmed our freezing skin.

A high-pitched giggle exploded on the deck below, and my head snapped to the source. My Treasure was staring into the sky, her chest shaking with her laughter as her clothes dried in the light.

Then, another laugh joined in, and another, until the entire crew was laughing with my *ĝha*. Even I was chuckling, though nothing about our battle against the sea was funny. We were giddy to be alive. We couldn't believe we made it.

Everyone began untying the knots at their waists, smiling into the sun and tangling with one another. The humans' knuckles were turning white as they clung to one another, their laughs turning to sobs of happiness. Unfreezing my feet from my spot, I began charging down the steps to my *ĝha*.

"Lookout!" Kovilu yelled. Looking back, an unseen wave brushed over the deck, swiping my *ĝha* straight over the edge.

Chapter Thirty-Five
Priscille

One moment, I'm standing on the deck celebrating our victory over the storm, and the next, I'm being yanked beneath the waves.

My eyes burn from the water, but I try to catch the direction of my breath before I lose it for good. As my lungs burn, I pump my legs and swing my arms, hoping I'm heading in the right direction. Yet, I still can't find the surface.

When my lungs feel like fire, panic sets in. Now, I'm not swimming; I'm thrashing, searching for light, trying not to pull in the breath my lungs desperately want.

I feel my hand breach the surface, and as my face comes up, I suck in a mouthful of water, coughing and choking on more. Another wave rolls over me, and I'm shoved backward beneath the water again. I'm choking up water, only for more to flood into my lungs. The harder I look for air, the worse the choking gets.

My arms and legs are spasming and flopping as I try to kick myself to the surface again, but before I can, another rolling wave drags me further down.

More water comes flooding into my body, and the last thing I see is blackness.

Chapter Thirty-six

Mekho

Priscille's tiny pale hand pierces the surface, and I dive into the water. From the moment she disappeared beneath the current, Kovilu rushed to drop the anchor, and we all searched for any sign of her. I was already tumbling toward the massive sea when a gasp came from the deck, pointing to the place I needed to be. Then, water collapsed around me, and I kicked deeper into the water.

The sunlight was still weak above me, but I opened my third eye, searching for her aura all around her. A bright golden light radiated from her body mere feet from me, and I used everything I had to reach her. Wrapping my arms around her body, I felt her drift limply through the water as my legs and tail swirled together, driving me to the surface. The ship was not too far, but even as we breached the surface, her chest did not begin a steady rise and fall.

Slinging her over my shoulder, I hurried up the ladder Kovilu and dropped into the water. Everyone waited beside the ladder as I took the last step, gently lowering her to the deck.

"I can help," Victoria spouts, pushing me to the side as she seals her lips to my *ĝha*'s and breathes air into her lungs forcefully. She repeats this process two more times, listening for a heartbeat and then compressing my *ĝha*'s chest. For the first time in my life, true panic settles inside me, and my hearts beat out of sync.

"Please, please, please," I whisper, watching as my *ĝha*'s chest rises and falls mechanically with Victoria's pace.

She pauses again, blowing into Priscille's mouth three more times. Her hands come to Priscille's chest, but my *ĝha* begins coughing and sputtering. Too much water explodes from her mouth, scattering onto the deck as Victoria helps her into a seated position. Priscille curls over herself as another round of water expels itself from her body.

I can't tell if it's ocean water or tears tracking down her face, but I don't care as I pull her into my chest. My hearts are still a frantic cacophony inside me, but I don't let her go. The relief in the group is nothing like the relief inside me. They almost lost a friend, not their other half, not the person who keeps the hearts in their chest beating. They would have survived the loss. I would not have.

"I'm okay," She says, looking up at me. Her voice is raw, and I hush her, rubbing a hand down her hair.

I can only imagine how I might look to her, squeezing her to me as if I must convince myself she is real, my eyes wide with color, silvery heat stinging at the base of my horns.

"I swear I'm alright, Mekho." She whispers against my chest.

Still, I cling.

Curse the ocean. Curse Vova. Curse being a sea warrior. I would take my *ĝha* to land, and I would never leave it again. My *ĝha* would love that.

I would build her a house with a garden and a chair for her to read outdoors. I would bring every ledger I ever filled inside and make her more from leather and leaves. She could write her own stories and fill shelves I'd build for her. I would gift her local flowers and special foods and make adventures from the land we lived on so we would never want to step on a ship again. When it would rain, I'd tuck her inside and wrap her in cozy linens until she didn't want to leave, and when we went to sleep at night, I would watch her chest rise and fall steadily. I would never take that for granted again.

"You are my everything," I whisper, breathing her in until I can scent the flowers beneath the salt. "I will love you even after Sheva calls me home."

Chapter thirty-seven
Priscille

Mekho doesn't leave my side after my near-drowning incident. Which is fine because I'm exhausted. The ocean gave me a beating, and Victoria's CPR may have saved me, but the bones in my chest ached, making breathing harder than it already was. Anytime I coughed, Mekho would rub a soothing hand down my back, and if I ever wanted to take a nap, he'd tuck me into his massive bed and guard me like an angel.

We were only a day from Wupeso now and past the Rough Waters. Mekho had decided we were safe enough to allow the humans free reign of the ship as long as they stayed out of the way of the crew as they worked. All that meant was humans became a helping hand. The children especially loved to learn about all the daily tasks and didn't mind shouting, "Swab the deck."

Being this close to the island, Buttercup could finally sense Blossom, and her attitude had improved a minuscule amount. After everything had happened during the storm, Jane had retreated to the bunks to check on the children and found Buttercup telling them to be silent or the wave monsters would get them – scarring them for life because she could.

Still, part of me was worried about landing in Wupeso. Even though Mekho stole me from the Valkarrans, the two villages were allied. If Serkha had returned before us, it would be likely Kano already knew about the situation. If a pirate ship pulled up to his cove, guns blazing, I wasn't sure we would be welcome, even with a cartful of new humans. Even two weeks ago, this wouldn't have mattered to me, but now...

Kano was an even-tempered, faithful man, and I had to believe he would listen to reason. It might not be a smooth transition. I had faith it would all work out.

Mekho's hand brushed back a lock of hair from my face, his eyes searching mine carefully, sniffing out any pain I might try to hide from him.

"What do you think about, Treasure? What secrets does your beautiful mind hide from me?"

I roll my eyes, catching his free hand and squeezing it gently. We were still in bed, even though it was well past time for him to relieve Niti from her duties. It didn't matter too much because Kovi would cover for him, and when he left, they would just send him back to guard over me again. But I heard Jajo and Ngheza joking about this being the reason you never let a man be captain, and it irked me to know the crew was picking on him. Mekho made a great captain.

"I'm working through what our arrival in Wupeso might look like. We went through this whole wild journey, and it might not even be over yet."

"I think our journey is much closer to an end than you know." He murmurs, placing a gentle kiss on my forehead.

That was another thing.

All I wanted to do was bask in the glory of our aliveness once we survived that storm. I was ready to jump Mekho's bones, or at least return all the favors he'd supplied me, but after the drowning episode, he wrapped me up tight and treated me like porcelain.

I enjoyed being his precious treasure, but all my leftover adrenaline had gone to complete waste. All my joy for being alive was squandered on good soups and conversations with the crew when they would let me out long enough to take a lap.

"There it is again, your mind working faster than a sea storm." His thumb brushes at the wrinkles in my forehead, and I force myself to soothe. "You know, when we have completed our *r̈ uṣad'ù*, you cannot hide your thoughts from me if I wish to pry."

"Will you pry often?"

"I would like to tell you 'no,' but I am a pirate. Stealing things is part of the job. Your mind is a treasure trove of things I long to steal and love."

"You're quite good at that." I agree; refusing to expand on what I mean because *you stole my heart* is too cheesy for even me.

A loud cawing sounds from outside, and Mekho perks up at the sound. Jajo and Ngheza must be in the nest when they yell in unison, "Land ahead!"

My eyes widen, and Mekho smirks.

"I told you we were closer than you thought. The storm actually hastened our journey, and Buttercup tailored our course."

"We're in Wupeso?"

"We're home, Priscille."

Chapter Thirty-Eight
Priscille

The crew holds the flag of surrender as we slog our way into the cove. Above me, Rihu and Royi spin about on their *uhichi* mounts, keeping their arrows trained on the ship. On land, more soldiers stand at the ready, and my worst fears are confirmed. Kano stands beside the water with Vera and her dragon-dog by her side.

Some humans gather behind the rows of soldiers, observing with the *peholoe* at their sides. I can see Aston, with Llazho two steps behind her. Daria and Demi stand together to the side, looking on with interest. Not Clara, though. A few of the Vòllø I know stand at the ready. Zhalisee is there with her apprentice, Hoga is dressed in beautiful armor I've never seen before.

Our ship hits the sand, and soldiers splash into the shallow water to scale the ship.

Mekho smirks in my direction, but his hands go to his sides, unlatching his weapons and dropping them to the deck. His crew follows his lead, and the clatter of metal on the wood makes me jump. The humans are all between me and the crew, nervously bouncing from foot to foot as we await orders from the village below.

"It's the pirate Kethi Rogeshu described," A man shouts down to Kano. I want to tell the Vòllø he's wrong because the pirate Kethi likely described was a scallywag who stole me from the Valkarrans. This pirate... Mekho was my *ĝha*.

"They've brought more humans!" Another man adds, his eyes roving over the survivors of the other escape pod. A shocked gasp echoes through the onlookers, and I remind myself what a blessing they will see this to be.

Vera leans over to whisper in Kano's ear, and he nods at whatever sage advice she's bestowed on him.

"Secure him and his crew. Escort the rest safely down," Kano orders. Vera's beast gnashes its teeth ferociously beside him, and I glance back at the children to ensure they are unafraid.

Carter stands tall, but the rest of the children seem nervous. For over a week now, this crew was the only Vòllø they knew, and they were about to be introduced to a whole lot more. The humans outnumbered the Vòllø on the ship, but that wasn't the case here in the village.

"You ready?" I ask the humans after they bring the crew from the ship.

A symphony of yeses met my ears.

Vera tugs me into a hug so tight I can barely breathe. She's a skinny little thing, but she wrings any leftover water from my weakened lungs.

"Jesus Christ, Priscille. We're so glad you're okay."

"I can tell," I smile, wrapping my arms around her to return the hug. Her beast, Magnus, growls after a few moments, and I step back. As Kano trails after the crew and toward the meeting hut, Vera stays with me and the humans. When she steps away from me, she smiles at everyone and asks for their names.

They introduce themselves, and I smile when Carter takes the liberty of introducing her entire family.

"I'm Carter Novak, that's my older sister Sadie Novak, and that's my mom. Her name is Jane, but we call her mama."

Jane's cheeks heat, and she places a hand on Carter's head to keep her from spouting more random facts about them all.

When the whole crew is introduced, Buttercup emerges from somewhere like the spook she is and says, "I'm Buttercup, the synthetic intelligence of escape pod two. Can you direct me to my sister, Blossom?"

This seems to surprise Vera, but the expression instantly drops from her face as she nods.

"Blossom recently returned from Valkarra. She will be in the *peholoe* loft, which is where I will take you."

The humans nod along, their eyes searching the surroundings. I try to remember what it was like for me when I first stepped onto the island. The floating islands above us were the most stunning thing to me, aside from the crystal fields I could see from the loft's edges. I was curious about them before I ever knew what they represented, and I loved the energy they gave me. Just being this close to them again made me want to run and pray, maybe while hugging one of the big red crystals tangled in tiny blue crystal flowers.

Our escape pod had landed in almost the same spot as our ship, and the welcome was a little different but equally as cautious. So, I know Kano is only doing his duty to protect his people.

Vera shuffles the people forward, leading the trek to the *peholoe* loft. As we hike along, she waves at people in town, telling the humans behind me their names and explaining the roles they fill. A farmer, a butcher, Zhalisee, the healer.

When we reach the bottom of the karst, Vera sighs deeply. She couldn't wait to stop taking the hike up the karst steps. We had barely been here a week when she started sleeping in Kano's bed on the ground. She wasn't scared of the steps like her best friend had been, but she didn't love the hike. To be honest, I didn't either.

"Hope you're not afraid of heights," She grumbles, taking the first step.

On our way to the *peholoe* loft, some humans gasp and point out special things about the island.

From the island's edge, you can see the gash in the land on the far side. I shiver when I remember Vera almost died falling to that crevasse. They point out the fields of shiny blue Helleboralis mushrooms and the crashing waterfall leading into the cove. Some children point out fancy plants on the ground, and a few glimpse the crystal fields.

"Wupeso is beautiful," Rashmi whispers, her eyes alight with joy.

As Vera waves us on, a few of us groan. "It's not much farther. I promise."

Then, the sprawling *peholoe* loft is there in the trees. Vera leads us around the corner and up through the ramp entry, and it's like I remember.

If Architect's Digest came to life in prehistoric times, this is what it would look like. Walls made of vented slats are opened to allow a natural cross breeze. Beautiful woods of easily replaceable wood are flat and glossy. Tatami-style mats and a low-to-the-ground, natural wood counter are to the left. A half-finished game of Neked'I sits straight in front of us, and the hall dips away in front of the kitchen area. In the back corner, a water feature made of rock tumbles and churns fresh water into a basin beneath it.

"This is where you've been staying?" Victoria blurts. Her eyes are wide as her neck curves to take it all in.

"Even better, it has a working bathroom. Let me show you," Vera adds, leading the serious woman away.

Soon enough, the soft chatter of the other women living in the *peholoe* loft fills my ears as they head down the hall. Heading toward the conversation, I find them all sitting along the edge of the bathing pool. Alba sees me first, pushing herself away from the water and wrapping me in her arms.

"We were so worried when we heard the news."

"I'm fine," I whisper, hugging the older woman back. "Better than fine, actually. Turns out the pirate had a reason to snatch me off Serkha's boat."

"It better be a good one," Vera chimes in, "Otherwise, Kano's going to rip him to shreds."

I break my hug with Alba to meet her eyes and say, "It's the best one. He's my *ĝha*."

Chapter Thirty-nine
Mekho

They separated me from my crew, dragged me into a musty building, and strapped me to the floor with metal latching contraptions. Now, I was waiting in the dark while the Rogeshu left to pray. He left me with two of his trusted sky warriors and an aching jaw.

At least I had entertainment. My shoulders ached from the position they were in, but I strained against my restraints anyway. Meanwhile, the two soldiers left to my care chatted as if they didn't have a care in the world.

"We must help Daria." One of them says, running a hand through his short, choppy hair.

"Demi says – "

"Demi is part of the problem."

The other warrior's jaw tenses at the words, but he's calm when he offers, "Or part of the solution. The lovely Daria loves her sister, but it has forced her to act as the younger girl's mother. Demi said to me she misses the old Daria."

"The *Earth* Daria," His companion spits.

They look so similar it's hard to catalog their differences – as long as they're not talking. One is clearly more impulsive than the other, and he heats as the discussion wears on.

"They need a family, Rihu."

"And you suppose it should be ours? Mine?"

This seems to injure the calmer of the two. His head snaps back as if he's been hit, and his tail twitches beneath him. It doesn't take him long to regain his composure, but as he's about to respond, steps sound outside the building.

Both soldiers come to attention, an unspoken agreement passing between them. Then, I'm standing in front of the one person I wished not to see.

The Valkarran Captain smiles in my direction, a step behind a tall Rogeshu. The Wupeson Rogeshu stands to the other's side, holding a tray of tinctures and torture devices. Outside, I see a fidgety healer's apprentice.

Both men step aside, allowing the captain through – Serkha. Priscille mentioned her in our many conversations.

She looked rested and confident. She spared only a momentary glance at the tray of implements before shooing it away. Brushing back her braids, she says, "Leave us."

Both Rogeshu and the soldiers from before duck out of the tent. She opens the glow lantern above me, bathing the room in light and making my eyes ache. My *jisa* feels weak, but I say nothing as she circles me. When she finally comes to a stop in front of me, she clucks her tongue in my direction.

"I used to know a woman who looked *just like you.* She was a pirate too, told me there were more lands beyond the Rough Waters, drew me maps too."

I know she speaks of my mother.

"I was never stupid enough to make those crossings, but when she did, she sought me out. She brought me goods from a place she called 'the mainland.' What do you know of that place?"

I swallow back my fear. Memories of the ship passing us by near the Rough Waters had my mouth dry. I wondered if they knew of this place like I did. I wondered if they would send their men here to pillage and plunder. Or worse, to force them into the mainland way of living.

"The mainland is the largest land I've ever found. Multiple villages are scattered across it. The Death of Baso Sheva hit them the worst. Only one woman remains, and she is ruling the lands and most of the surrounding islands."

Rumor had it she was a mother to monsters, a slave to darkness, but I'd never come close enough to her to confirm or deny. I also don't talk about how she sends untested men on expeditions to expand her reign or that she killed her *ĝha* when he appeared. As far as I heard, she considered herself part of the goddess – not a mere triplicate but a quad, to live upon Shojo and exercise their will over men. Every man on the mainland either adored her or could not escape her clutches.

Serkha nods, her hand coming to rest on my chest. My marks flare at her unwelcome touch, and I snarl. She smiles, backing away.

"When I saw your ship, I thought you were a mainlander coming for my crew. Your mother was not at the helm but a man. I thought you would take Priscille and return for more humans. I was only trying to protect her."

"So, you tried to keep her from me because you thought I would what? Sell her to the mainland?"

Serkha nods, and my hearts drop.

"Has this happened before?" I ask, wondering if she had lost crew members to mainlander pirates, wondering if they were finding Vòllø women across the lands to sell, wondering what the mainland was doing with them.

"My crew and I have been sinking any ships that make it across the Rough Waters, but as you've proven, we can't catch them all."

Disbelief and disgust war in my chest, and all I want now is to see my *ĝha*. I needed to lay eyes on her, bond her to me, and protect us with a lifelong connection blessed by the true Baso Sheva. I needed to do all of that and then build her the house of her dreams and pledge myself to defend it.

Serkha seems to see the truth of my hearts in my eyes because she nods.

"You will see your *ĝha* soon, pirate. But first, the Rogeshu have questions."

Chapter Forty

Priscille

I can feel the moment Clara enters the *peholoe* loft like a prickle across my skin. Something about my friend spoke to my soul, and I left the bathhouse with surprising speed.

"Priscille?" She calls as I make my way around the corner. She's standing at the ramp entrance with one hand against the end of the wall and another against –

"King Solispera?" I question, eyeing the winged man.

"Human Priscille," He replies, bowing his head.

Shaking out my surprise, I find my way to Clara, wrapping her in my arms. I squeeze so hard her breath is an 'oof' at my ear, but when her arms come around me, she gets her revenge. Her tiny arms are secret pythons as she strangles me with her love.

"Heavens, I missed you."

"I missed you, too." She whispers back, holding me tightly. "I can't believe you got stolen by a pirate."

"I can't believe that pirate is my *ĝha*."

She stiffens in my arms, breaking away slightly. Her smile is wide as she exclaims, "Really?"

"Would I lie to you?"

Pulling me through the room, she navigates us to the mats along the floor before capturing both my hands in hers and saying, "Tell me everything."

I spent the next two hours telling her the entire story, how he stole me from Serkha's ship, how we had to share my earbud for days, and how the crew didn't trust me, but I pushed myself to learn the language and become their friends, how we found the pod on our way to get married in the mainland, and how he changed his plans for me and the humans even though he knew he wouldn't be well-received here. I even kiss and tell a little to gush about his devotion.

"Wow, three times? I bet the sex was amazing after," She says, wiggling her eyebrows slightly.

"Uhm. Well… Wekindofhaven'thadsexyet."

"What?" She says, "I know I can't see, but I think it must be affecting my hearing because I thought you said you haven't had sex with him yet."

"We're waiting for our *r̈ uṣad'ù*."

The realization dawns on her. "Oh my god. You never made it to the mainland," Her ears practically steam at the work her mind does. "You've been sleeping in his bed for weeks without a single touch, a single look?"

"A single look at what?" Aston asks, finding a seat beside us.

"The pirate's dick," Clara answers for me, making me choke on the air.

"Clara," I reprimand. At the same time and in the same tone, Aston says, "Priscille."

Deeming this an emergency, the redhead finds her seat beside us and joins the conversation. Aston was the kind of woman who believed she belonged in every circle, and if I was honest, she did. She always knew exactly how to infiltrate a situation.

Taking one of my hands from Clara's, I tilt my head to look in Aston's direction, "I need you to understand, I hate Llazho, but I've seen his dick."

She steals the air from my lungs with her admission, and I can hear Abbess Carlow in my mind. *Sin. Vile, vile sin. That woman needs to go to confession.*

"It's not that I haven't had the opportunity. I just haven't looked."

"What if he's malformed?"

I can feel the blush on my cheeks. I know Mekho's not malformed. He's entirely too cocky about it to be malformed, but I don't say so. I can't get the words past my lips.

"This needs immediate action. Where is the pirate? You should go to him now. Tell him to drop his drawers." Aston demands, "An eager beaver eater is one thing, but you have to know the truth of his dick. If only so you know you can handle it. These guys are huge."

Though Clara's own cheeks are pink, she nods, "I have to agree, Pris."

I sigh. "That's all great and dandy, but the man's kind of arrested under guard right now for stealing me from the Valkarrans."

Clara pats my knee, "Easy enough to fix. I'll tell Roxie it's an emergency for you to see him, and she will tear Kethi a new one if he doesn't let it happen."

I look to Aston, and she's nodding enthusiastically, "I'm the leader of the Mate-Hate club, but we all love Kethi."

Clara holds out her left hand, and suddenly, King Solispera is there, helping her to her feet. His head ducks to her ear, and he whispers something that makes her blush. Then, he straightens and leads us all to where they're keeping my *ĝha.*

Chapter Forty-one
Mekho

The Rogeshu asked me a hundred different questions about where I found the humans, the condition of the escape pod, and whether I knew the location of any others. They ask me about why I endangered Priscille to bring her across the Rough Waters, not once but twice. I keep it to myself that I had to cross it three times to even make that happen. Nor do I tell them the first two times were smooth sailing. Then, they decide how to punish me.

"We should forbid you from seeing her." Kano Rogeshu argues.

I would escape my bonds and kidnap her again before I allowed that to happen. Priscille spoke of Kano as a reasonable, faithful man, but something about my behavior has enraged him. Now, he wishes to keep me from my *ĝha*.

"He has *ĝha* marks," Serkha explains.

After our first set of questions, I decided I liked the Valkarran Captain. She was truly reasonable, knew my mother, and had seen my crew. My story corroborated theirs perfectly. She said I was "honest for a pirate."

"Yes, but does she?" Kethi Rogeshu asks.

My eyes narrow to pins on the Valkarran Rogeshu. I try to tell him with my eyes that I will tear his tongue from his mouth for his comment. But a short woman with silken black hair bursts into the room with my *ĝha* two steps behind her. The woman folds her arms across her chest as she glares at the man. Her words are heavens heard.

"She does. And she needs a moment, everyone out."

I watch with fascination as the soldiers and leaders flee from the room at her command, leaving me chained to the floor in front of my *ĝha*.

Priscille looks incredible. Her lips are a darker pink than usual, and it reminds me of the gift I have hidden away for her. She wears a dress I have not seen her in before, but I like it. Instead of the common linen threads, this one is layers and layers of sheer and floaty fabric. Soft waves of her hair cascade down her back, and she fiddles with her fingers like she's nervous. My Jewel takes a deep breath and drags her eyes from the floor to meet mine.

Her slight gasp reminds me I probably look foolish. I'm sure there's some slight bruising, making me look more gray than blue, and the dust in the room has seemed to invade my clothes, which are all askew from being pushed around. Meanwhile, she looks like she's ready for our *r̈uṣad'ù*.

"Come to bust me out of here, Treasure?"

Her cheeks pinken in the way I love, but she tilts her head to the left to say no. Her nerves seem to relax a little, and I push a little harder.

"To steal a kiss then?"

Her golden-brown eyes roll in their sockets, but her smile grows wider. The pinkness on her cheeks remains firmly in place, and I smirk in her direction. In several bounding steps, she reaches me, standing on the tips of her toes to kiss me. I have to strain against my bindings to reach her, but it's all worth it when I do.

Her lips touch mine, and a small bolt of energy bursts across my *jisa*. The tender caress of her lips makes the world beyond this room fade into the background. This stolen moment between us reminds me we are still unbonded, even though my hearts beat for her. Before I can beg for her to strengthen the unseen thread between us, her lips break from mine.

"The girls sent me in here because they say I'm unprepared for our *r̈ ůṣad'ù*."

My brows wrinkle, a smirk still on my face. "Having second thoughts, Treasure?"

"Not at all. I'm here, so the women stop asking about the size of," She pauses, cheeks heating again, "It doesn't matter. I'm not here to investigate, just to make it seem like I did."

My smirk grows into a full-grown smile, "I don't mind, Priscille. You can do whatever *investigation* you need to."

She pushes against my chest, stepping away, and I curse my bindings. I miss her hands on me already.

"Roxie and Vera are going to talk to the Rogeshu," Priscille says instead, "If all goes well, we can marry, *bond*, at sunset tomorrow."

She's still standing a touch too far from me, but I beckon her closer with my straining. My head tilts towards hers, and I capture her lips once again. Then, I whisper against her ear, "Can't wait."

Chapter Forty-two
Priscille

"Don't trust a word they say about the *r̈uṣad'ù* being no big deal," Roxie shouts, breaking into the bathhouse as I prepare for my *r̈uṣad'ù*. She looks as tough as her pointed violet nails and elegant too in her silky black dress that has a slit to mid-thigh. Vera enters right behind her, looking like a supermodel. Her wide-leg linen pants and cropped shirt make her appear taller than she already is and accentuate her tiny waist.

"Roxie's right. He'll tell you it's no big deal, and then you'll have to face down a dragon without the use of your eyes."

Wrapping one arm carefully over my chest, I point to my towel outside the water. Roxie huffs, holding it out for me as she tilts her head away.

"Modest as a nun," She grumbles.

"She is a nun," Vera reminds her.

"I'm not a nun," I protest. "I was *thinking* about becoming a nun."

Roxie snorts, "Could've fooled me."

Wrapping the towel around my body, I do my best to imitate her as I glare in her direction.

"Roxie, be nice. It's her wedding day."

"No, it's her *r̈uṣad'ù*. She needs to be on her A-game."

"It won't be that bad," I say, regret churning my stomach as their heads snap toward mine.

"That bad?" Vera asks.

"That bad?" Roxie echoes. "Kethi almost died. If Ijigan didn't find me, I would have had to carry Kethi down the mountain *on top of a porcu-wolf.*"

I cringe at her words. It was true; Roxie and Vera had been through the ringers with their *r̈uṣad'ù*. I mean, I had to physically evacuate Roxie's ceremony so I didn't die by evil space spider. And Vera has the scariest pet I've ever seen, thanks to hers. Yet, something in my heart told me that almost drowning, navigating the Rough Waters, and facing the anger of the village earned me a little peace during my ceremony.

Before I left Mekho's prison yesterday, we discussed the sound plan. We would navigate the caves together, deal with whatever Baso Sheva threw at us, emerge together and exchange our vows, and then kiss in front of the village and crew. There would be no staying for the celebration. We would immediately retreat to the ship and seal the fresh new bond as a couple should. No pet-retrieval, no healers necessary.

Vera's arm comes around my shoulder in a half-hug. She whispers, "Don't let Roxie's drama tear you down. I'm sure you will be fine, no matter what happens."

Roxie's eye-roll was felt around the world.

"C'mon. Let's get you ready for your swashbuckling *ĝha,*" Vera says, leading me out of the bathhouse. As she leads me into the main area of the *peholoe* loft, I'm relieved to see it's only women.

With Vera's *r̈uṣad'ù* we all decided one tradition from Earth we were keeping was the women getting together before the ceremony. For Vera, Aston organized a whole party for the night before, and for Roxie, the girls who stayed in Valkarra spent the morning helping her get ready. It seemed mine would be a cross between the two.

Part escape pod mixer, part get ready with me party, there were women all over the loft preparing for my ceremony and chatting back and forth. As I emerged, Aston caught my eye, announcing my arrival loudly. A small round of cheers and smiles come my way, and then I'm guided to a spot beside Clara.

"Having fun yet?" She asks, swinging her fingers through the air until she can feel mine.

"This is crazy, right?" I ask, turning to face her. "I mean, it's crazy to marry a man who kidnapped me a month ago, right?"

"On Earth, sure. Here, I'd say it's a normal day." Clara responds, giving my fingers a comforting squeeze.

My heart clenches in my chest, and I whisper, "I knew August for years, and I still didn't know who he was. What if I'm doing that to myself again?"

"Would Mekho hurt you?" She asks, her other hand reaching out for me. I take it in my free hand and try not to tap my foot with panic.

Mekho didn't even hurt me when I thought I deserved it, and he became a wreck when I'd been hurt.

"No, he wouldn't hurt me."

I remember his words when I told him of August. He told me he would do anything to earn my trust, and he did. Since that moment, he had proved in every action he took he trusted me, and I could trust him, too. The look in his eyes when I described August's abuse was one of pure hatred.

"Even if he did, you would have me. You would have the rest of the Vòllø. On Earth, things can get bad, and no one knows. Here, you would come to me with a bruise, and

I would have a pack of rabid men at my back to fight for your honor."

"I mean, they're letting me marry a pirate."

"No, you want to marry a pirate. And that's great, Pris." Before I can protest any further, Clara is asking for my dress and running her hands through my hair. "Now, what does my bride want? Half-up, half-down? A big chop?"

"I want one long, beautiful braid."

"I can arrange that."

Chapter Forty-three
Mekho

Slivers of the Sun Earlier

"It's perfect," I say, looking over the single-room structure on the land. People in Wupeso abandoned homes and partial buildings like this one completely during the Death of Baso Sheva and started living in group living spaces instead. One of these abandoned buildings was a tiny circle hut with a single support beam at its center. It was on the edge of the cove, in the karst's shade. It would bring us close to the crystal fields for morning prayers, close to the *peholoe* loft where the human women and most of my crew would take up residence. The view of the waterfall was magnificent, and it was close to the cove, so I could watch my ship come and go without me.

"It's a dump," Kovilu spouts beside me. Her words bring a smirk to my face.

The grass surrounding the structure is half as tall as the structure itself, and the musty scent of wood left to rot in the brush permeates the area, but otherwise, it's perfect.

"You have to imagine it as it will be, not what it is," I explain. I paint Kovi a picture of the home I see with my words. "From the tiny circle hut, I'd add a large rectangle space off the back to fill with rooms for children. I'd treat all the wood with the tar we used for our ships to offset the mist from the cove and waterfall. On the far side, I'll lay out some sand and stone and make a big chair for Priscille to sit in.

"You will live right over there, in the house that's perfectly built and beautiful already. You can live by yourself or the other crewmates to share, but you have to be down here because this is a family plot of land, and you're my family."

The color drains from Kovi's eyes, and I force strength into my *jisa*. Her head snaps to the empty home only a few paces away and then back to the tiny hut I planned to fix.

"Have you already spoken with Kano Rogeshu?"

"And Pa *Peholoe* and the crew. They all agree it's best if I give up the pirate's life and put down new roots for Priscille. Make a proper home for us all."

The sound of shuffling grass begins behind us, and I look over my shoulder to see those people. Pa leads my crew and a group of Wupesons forward through the grass with a smile on his face. They carted in sleds filled with materials, and after explaining my vision, we all got to work.

Chapter forty-four
Priscille

Pa beams as he leads me, blindfolded, through the caves. He puts me in some little alcove somewhere, whispers the holy words, and then his steps retreat. Standing there alone, I worry I won't be able to do this. Vera and Roxie both caught up with me after I was dressed to give me some pointers, but I got confused about the whole 'talk mind to mind' thing.

Then, I hear some steps approaching, and my fears melt away. I'm not sure how I know it's Mekho, whether it's the cadence of his walk or his soothing salt and rum scent, but I know it's my *ĝha*. He finds me, and I hear his soft exhalation. It's tinged with relief, and the experience feels like coming home.

"Take my hand, Priscille."

I seek it from behind the blindfold and gasp when our hands meet. Suddenly, I can see myself through Mekho's eyes. Encased in an aura of warm gold and orange tones, I stand in the wedding dress my friends created for me. My hair is a stunning braid woven through with crystal pins and flowers. His rumbling chuckle vibrates through me, and I hear his voice in my mind.

"I promised you I'd steal your thoughts, didn't I?"

Even in my mind, his voice is like peanut butter chocolate candies. Even in my mind, he sounds like a miracle.

"How can I do this?"

"It's our bond."

"But we're not even finished with the ceremony."

"The ceremony isn't what bonds us, ĝha."

Our connection separates as he tugs me out of my alcove. I trust him as he leads me blindly through the tunnels, but as we reach the tunnel leading out, he stops in his tracks.

His voice is reverent when he whispers, "It's a water spirit."

Allowing me back into his head, I can see the creature through his eyes. Glowing and blue, it reminds me of the will o' wisp tales. It's a little orb that looks kind of like a swirling droplet of water, but it floats about six feet off the ground.

"Will we have to kill it?" I ask, wondering how we would even do such a thing.

"No, I don't think so. It has something to tell us," Mekho replies, bringing us a step closer.

I realize then that I trust him implicitly. He could have led me toward danger, shoved me into some crazy beast, and lied about what we would face in these caves, but he did none of that. Mekho was honest with me, even when I wasn't honest with myself. Yes, he teased, and he joked, but it was never to cause harm. His humor was one reason I loved him.

I could feel his smirk rise on his face as he whispered, "Only one, huh? Guess I'm not trying hard enough."

We take another step toward the water spirit, and I can feel the prickle of unease enter my body. We've come close enough.

It speaks, and somehow, we both understand it.

"May I speak upon you a blessing?" The sprite-like creature asks.

We both nod our answer rather than speak, and I watch through Mekho's mind.

"May your hearts be fluid and steadfast in challenge. May your love be tranquil like the waters of peace. May your trust be as strong as the mightiest wave. Go forth blessed, Child of Baso Sheva and Child of God in your union from hereto and on."

I do the sign of the cross, and Mekho copies my movements, endearing me to him further. Then, we watch as the water spirit disappears into the mist.

Mekho leads me from the cave, whispering his vows like prayers in my ear.

"I promise to never squander our blessings, to always keep you safe, and keep you laughing. But most of all, I promise I will love you even after Baso Sheva steals me from this world."

I let his reasons sink into me and seal the cracks of my past. Then, I take a deep breath and make my own promises.

"On Earth, in my religion, these are the promises I would make.

"I, Priscille Amadori, take you, Mekho Wogo, to be my husband. To have and to hold, from this day forward, for better or worse, for richer, for poorer..."

I make a tiny change, "As long as our souls are bound."

I can feel his emotions run through me like they are my own, and he leads me from the cave with new vitality. As we make it to the mouth of the cave, cheers and whoops and hollers erupt. The humans call for us to kiss, and Mekho does not disappoint.

Chapter forty-five

Mekho

Energy courses across my *jisa* as my lips land on hers. My hand unties her blindfold, and when I pull her against my chest, breaking our kiss, her eyes sparkle beneath the moonlight. Everyone cheers for our new bond, and I sweep her into my arms, carrying her past the crowd and out of the crystal fields.

My hearts are so full they're practically bursting. This kind of rush is completely new to me. Not even my biggest scores upon the sea felt this extraordinary. It was like my body was indestructible like I had fortified my mind in iron. I knew with certainty nothing could hurt me now, that my *ĝha* would forever be safe with me by her side because I had the power of Baso Sheva behind me.

Hustling down the path to our home, I keep my eyes on Priscille – and the trail. There is confusion in her eyes when I head toward our new place, but I simply mutter, "Short path."

She nestles into my chest, and my hearts squeeze. I have no idea what a plundering pirate like me did to earn such a respectable woman, but I trusted Baso Sheva's judgment. I would not question it further.

As I come over the hill, I see again, and it's like the first time. We cut down the grass, built the basic frame for the back part of the house, and moved our limited things into the part that was already standing. With the help of Jack and Ian, we put some doors on, and suddenly, there was a place for me to bring my perfect *ĝha* directly after our *r̈uṣad'ù*.

"What's this?" She asks, looking at our tiny patch of land. Just beyond the back of the house, a waterfall tumbles for measures and measures into the cove, misting on the rocks below and catching the light of the silver moon above us. The slatted windows had been opened, and all the hundreds of glow crystals I'd collected illuminated the space.

"This is our home."

Her startled look brings a smirk to my face, and I walk her up to the door.

"But I thought the ship was our home."

"No, my darling Treasure. You are my home. The ship was just a residence. This is just a residence. But I hope to make it the perfect residence for you."

Opening the door, I swing us inside. It's even better than I first imagined. My bed lay on the far wall, our bedside tables stacked high with knick-knacks from my travels and tiny glowing crystals. The woven red rug is against the back door, which will eventually lead to the other wing of the home, and my desk sits on the other side of it.

Setting her on the floor, I watch as she checks it out. Below deck, I'd kept a bunch of things hidden away for a moment like this. I hadn't known it then, but the cushioned pillows I stole from a Tsache warrior and the leftover *rid'i* plants our supplier refused to buy that I refused to throw out were the perfect decorations. Even better, an outdated map I found makes the perfect wrapping for her gift.

After she surveys the room, she spins to face me. I hold out the tiny box. She's familiar with what's inside, but she doesn't know that yet.

"A gift?"

"For you."

Her tiny fingers take the box from my hand, and her caress across my skin makes my *jisa* shake. Slowly tearing

163

away the paper, I wait with anticipation as she catches sight of the tiny wooden box.

"Seeds?" She asks. Her nose wrinkles with her confusion, and I urge her to open the box further.

When she finally does, her mouth drops open, and her eyes widen. Her fingers shake as she pulls the pink stone from the box.

"It's a cross," she whispers reverently, pulling the charm from the box until the thin silver chain is no longer among the sawdust inside. "It's incredible."

As her feelings flood my body, I harden. Her peace, and love, and gratitude all ran through my veins like a sea of happiness.

"The man I bought it from said it would protect my home," I mention, watching her lift it over her head. She pauses momentarily before slipping it the rest of the way on.

"Home is where we are, right?"

I give her one of my genuine smiles because she is absolutely right.

Chapter forty-six

Priscille

Every time Mekho comes within touching distance, my body revs up with need. When he smirks, I want to kiss the smug look off his face. When he laughs, I want it to be because of something I said. When his hands come around my hips and graze my sides, I want more.

The glow of the crystals makes the light around our new home low and romantic. He's crouched in front of me, and I stand between his legs and the beautiful necklace he got for me hangs around my neck as I rub my fingers over the cool stone, and he doesn't even know how significant of a gift it is. He doesn't know how validating it is to see. If I had any doubt in Baso Sheva or God, it was gone now because it took both of them to bring me here to this moment. To get *us* to this moment.

Our eyes meet. The necklace drops from my hands, falling against my breastbone. My eyes trace across the sharp lines of Mekho's jaw, searching the shadows cast by the light. Then, I bend to kiss him at the same moment he surges up to meet me.

His hands tighten on my hips as he picks me up from the floor. My dress slides up my thighs as my legs wrap his waist, and I can feel the head of his cock, hot and hard beneath my core. His tongue brushes my lip, and I open on a gasp.

He takes mere seconds to reach the bed, eating up the room with his long strides as I grind against him. He wraps one arm around my hips, and we tumble onto the sheets. Our kiss breaks as his hands shimmy my dress off, leaving it in a pile beside our bed.

My hands reach for his trousers as his eyes roam my body. Under his stare, I always feel invincible. He studies the curves and divots of my body like they're a map to the fountain of youth. His eyes don't leave mine until my hand wraps around his cock. Or tries to anyway. I grip his cock tight in my hand, but my fingertips can't quite touch. Mekho throws his head back with a groan as I squeeze.

My eyes are wide at his size, and I regret my decision not to see it before. My single previous lover was well-endowed, according to my understanding of anatomy, but this was *huge*. I feel myself clenching on air. His same indigo color becomes inky over the bulbous head, and a bright teal vein cuts a pattern across him in a pattern I wanted to follow with my tongue.

"Priscille," Mekho groans, a hint of warning in his tone. My eyes snap to his, and they're blown wide with color, locked onto the spot where my hand meets his cock. The contrast of my skin against his in such an intimate way has a low heat curling inside me.

Tentatively, I stroke him, watching his face morph with pleasure. A sense of power fills me, and I use it to fuel my bravery. With my hand around the base, I lean forward and guide my tongue along the vein. The muscles of Mekho's leg flinch as he holds himself in place. The pure awe written on his face bolsters my confidence. So, when I reach the head of his cock, I swirl my tongue around it before sucking it into my mouth.

I feel his shuddering breath as his hand comes to my head, guiding his cock further into my mouth. Hollowing my cheeks, I let him thrust while words of praise tumble from his lips.

"Treasure, you're perfect. Oh, yes. I love your hot little mouth on my cock."

Satisfaction rolls through me as his cock twitches inside my mouth. I'm a little out of practice, but keeping my lips locked around him, I can feel how close he is, so I flick my tongue against a spot right beneath the head, and then he's coming. Breathy groans tumble from his lips, and I feel him twitch against my tongue.

"That's it, *ĝha*. Take it for me."

Sucking his cock further into my mouth, I feel the first jet of liquid hit my tongue. He's a little salty in the best way, and I hum about him as I swallow.

Still hard when he slips from my mouth, Mekho bends to kiss me like I'm a gift from heaven.

His hands come around my face, and his eyes meet mine when he says, "You should know by now I'm going to make you come that hard on my tongue. But later, because right now I want to be inside you."

"Don't you need a second to recover?" I ask, glancing down to find him hard and waiting.

Mekho only smirks at me. "Do you?"

"Well, no."

"Then be my perfect Priscille, and watch as my cock sinks into your beautiful pussy."

My lashes flutter as he presses against my entrance, but I keep my eyes locked on the point where our bodies meet. His fist is pressed into the mattress beside my hip as he slowly glides into my body. And I'm honestly shocked at how greedily my body pulls him in. He's absolutely stretching me to my limits, but it means I can feel every tiny ridge of his cock as it presses into me. When there's only an inch or so more to go, I'm sure I won't be able to take any more.

Then, his thumb brushes my clit, and I arch into him, feeling the tiny bumps at the top of his pelvis grind against my sensitive center.

He pauses inside me, stilling my hips with his hands, and I moan. I want to squirm, feel him move inside me, but he doesn't let me.

"Look at me, Treasure."

I don't hesitate.

"Now tell me what you want."

My cheeks heat at all the naughty thoughts running through my head. So many filthy things, but all I want is for him to make love to me. I want him to hold me close and bring me to the edge with him. I want to come with him deep inside me.

"I want you to fuck me, deep but gentle. To look you in the eyes when we come."

He groans at my words, capturing my lips with his. His hips draw back, and I moan into his mouth. Then, he drives them forward with purpose, bottoming out with a slow grind against my clit. With his next thrust, I meet his movements, swirling my hips against him to feel the sparks of pleasure race across my skin.

"You're so tight." He murmurs, caging me against the bed beneath us.

"You're so *big*," I whisper right back, whimpering in his ear as he drives me closer and closer to the edge.

"Are you going to come for me, Priscille?" He drives into me with that same steady pace. I can feel his cock dragging along my G-spot. The tension inside me is winding tighter and tighter with each thrust and grind.

"Yes," I moan.

"Good, because I want to feel you squeezing around my cock. Your pussy begging for my come deep inside you. You want me to come inside you?"

"Yes," I moan again, feeling my approach to the edge. His eyes lock onto mine, and I feel myself flutter around him. His adoration is plain on his face.

"Then come for me, *ĝha*. Come on my cock."

He finishes his last thrust with his words, and I feel myself tilt over the edge. I spasm around his cock, moaning his name while I chant a chorus of yeses. He grinds against my swollen pussy as I do, coming over the edge with me. I feel him come deep inside me, and I feel so close to him that I want to cry.

"Sheva bless me. You're perfect," Mekho whispers, kissing my forehead and cheek, gathering me close to him as we come down together. "I love you, Priscille."

"I love you, too."

Chapter forty-seven
Mekho

Three Moons Later

"A *crib*?" Kovilu asks, her confusion matching my own. "What is this *crib*?"

"It is like a small wooden prison for the child's bed to lie in," I explain, eating from the plate of fruit she set out. We're seated on a blanket in the grass overlooking the cove. The ship is out there, tied next to a smaller fishing vessel bobbing on the water. Priscille is inside, sleeping. She was so ill this morning it wore her out.

"But why? I'm sure even a half-Vòllø child could escape such a flimsy thing."

"I have asked such things myself, but Zhu swears it is necessary for *nesting*."

Zhu was the only other Vòllø who had a pregnant human *ĝha*, so we had been speaking a lot recently.

Kovilu's nose wrinkles at the term *nesting*, and I admit I am happy to know the confusion isn't only my own. Though we did not expect children so soon, Priscille and I at least had the good sense to speak of them before it happened. We agreed we wanted children whenever Baso Sheva and her God gifted us with them. Now, my poor Priscille has been sick for two months, and all the human women swear it's a normal part of the process.

"So, she wants a wooden prison for your babe. What else? A torture device?" Kovi asks, reaching for our shared snacks.

"Nothing so harmful, just confusing. Apparently, Zhu has been frantic trying to organize something called a *baby shower*."

"Like a small tub for you to wash your child in?"

"Like a get-together where the women of the village bring the baby gifts before it is born, like clothes and toys. That is another thing. Priscille wants special toys for the child."

"It sounds like you will become quite the carpenter over the coming moons."

I sigh, my gaze tilting back toward our home. I had finished the addition, furnished the space, and brought in the proper water supply, and it was exactly as I imagined. My porch had a small chair that rocked back and forth. Priscille had sewn a small cushion for the seat, and as I glanced back now, she was seated in it.

She wasn't looking my way. Her face is stuffed into one of the many blank ledgers I gave her. She had a tiny quill with ink, and she was furiously scribbling notes in her human script to document her pregnancy. She had been keeping track of everything since we found out.

"Looks like you ought to head home now. Your *ĝha* will need you," Kovi says, standing from our spot. She waves at Priscille, and I watch my *ĝha* smile in our direction, waving goodbye. I tangle with Kovi before she leaves, thanking her for the time spent.

Then, I gather the blanket and walk toward my *ĝha*. Priscille recently began to bubble at her belly, and I rush the last few steps to help her from her chair as I approach. Her arms come around me, and mine around her. The house was ready, I'd build her crib, and when the child came, my home would grow because sometimes home wasn't about where you were, but who you were with.

Chapter – Epilogue

Daria

Fuck the *SS Herculean* for being overrun by aliens. Fuck the escape pod for landing here. And, most of all, fuck Commander Roxie Holt for being my first patient and putting me on Zhalisee's radar. It's all her fault I'm on my way to my *third* appointment of the day rather than finding my way off this planet. It's her fault I'm exhausted.

I sneak through the tall grass past Priscille's place to take the beach over to Cerridwen's instead of the primary thoroughfare. Since Zhu is a sky guy like Kano, he prefers the cliffside, and he moved Cerridwen into his place across the chasm bridge as soon as she let him. Which was apparently mere seconds after they met since we had only been on this planet for six Shojo months, and she was getting close to popping out the first half-Vòllø, half-human baby.

That was the reason for my visit. Since Cerridwen was the first mommy to an alien, she needed practically constant supervision. If it wasn't me going to check on her, it was Zhalisee or Blossom. Even if it was me going to check on her, half the time, I'd find another one there. Blossom was so curious about the science of the whole thing that she was constantly taking tiny blood samples and comparing them to the normal human pregnancy data she'd been trained on. And Zhalisee liked to pass on Vòllø tradition tidbits to connect with the patient.

With all three of us working together, we had learned a lot. So far, we learned she was likely well into her third trimester. The Vòllø gestation rate was slightly faster than the humans – according to our comparative calculations. Add to that the longer day/night cycle on Shojo, and we were swiftly approaching her deadline. By which I mean it could be any day. Any hour.

We also learned her child would most likely come out with tiny little baby horns that would start soft, grow and twist, and harden with age. The baby might have an extra organ called a *jisa,* and the baby has a thirty-two percent chance of killing Cerridwen throughout the birth process. *Thanks for the information, Blossom.*

Still, Zhu and Cerridwen weren't worried. They believed that no other place in the universe could provide better medical care. Their 'team' comprised me, a nurse who did a stint in OB; Zhalisee, who has birthed pretty much every Vòllø younger than her in the village; and Blossom, who could run tests for important things like gestational diabetes. We made up their *perfect* team. Cerridwen often said we took care of everything, so all they had to do was love one another.

I'm deep in my head, wondering if I should prescribe her something for delusion, as I step onto the beach. So I don't notice the two giant sky warriors headed my way.

"Darling Daria, have I ever told you you're my favorite of the humans?" Royi spouts, taking my medical kit from me. At first, that tiny gesture bothered me, but I've come to understand it's his love language. Whenever they caught up with me, Royi would carry my kit. He actually did a lot for me when he could, like delivering my groceries or helping me collect Demi's clothes from the drying lines.

"If he hasn't, let me be the first to tell you instead. You are my favorite human, Daria." Rihu greets. The color in his left eye flashes from its usual green to a dark forest color and back. The first time it happened, I thought he was having a stroke – which he ate up, by the way – but really, he winked at me.

"Where are you headed?" Royi asks, tearing my attention from the other warrior.

173

Rihu and Royi are like brothers. They're *not* brothers, which helps the unwanted attraction I've developed for them. But they *act* like brothers. They're best friends who bicker constantly. Royi calls Jaye 'mom,' even though she's actually just Rihu's mom. And they look incredibly similar. Like Demi and I look like siblings – we share our kinky curls and our disposition for dark clothes mostly – but it's easy to tell us apart. Rihu and Royi are like twins, which is why they have that moniker from the human women. Well, all the human women except me.

"Cerridwen's place. Another checkup."

Royi's pistachio brows furrow, and Rihu gives a sharp tilt of his head. That was another thing; they still had that weird twin telepathy thing going on. We were reaching the end of the beach soon, and I'd have to join the main path through town again to cross the bridge.

"We're lucky to have such a beautiful healer in our village," Rihu says with a smile. He grabs my wrist and twirls me in a circle before his hands fall to my waist. He lifts me over the sandy drop and onto the path.

I was fairly average in size with a full figure, but the man lifted me as if I were light as a feather. His arms barely even flexed, which was a pity. I loved watching his arms flex. It was why I watched them train their mounts when I got a spare moment – something I probably wouldn't have for another few days.

"It's perfect for when Rihu inevitably says something stupid and runs into Llazho's fist," Royi teases. I roll my eyes at their antics.

Anytime I was between them, it was like this. They would riff off each other, flirting with me in the sweetest ways. They loved to praise me for my healing and ask inappropriate questions about it, too. One time, Rihu asked if it was truly human custom to kiss an injury better. When I told him there was no medical science behind that, Royi told me that was unfortunate because he had a cut on his lip that could use some healing.

Something about the two of them made me forget I didn't want to be here, and that was dangerous.

Snagging my bag from Royi's arms, I reached up to grab his horn. He's thoughtful, so he leans down to allow the tangle before stepping back so I can do the same for Rihu. Rihu does *not* lean down for me, instead smirking in my direction as my body plasters to his during our tangle. As I'm sliding away, he sneaks a forehead kiss in.

"As always, it's a pleasure, Daria the Lovely," Royi says with a smile.

"Maybe one day it will be our pleasure," Rihu adds with a wink.

I roll my eyes, ignoring the two of them as I step into Zhu's home. I can hear Cerridwen's frantic breathing from the other room, and I hurry through the curvy maze. She's glowing – in that awful pregnancy sweat kind of way – and panting on her bed. Zhu's brows are almost a knot on his forehead, and Buttercup, the less friendly version of Blossom, is standing off to the side of the room.

"I'm having contractions. I think I'm going to go into labor," Cerridwen says, groaning through some pain.

"She is wrong. It's Braxton Hicks," Buttercup says, "But she won't believe me. Blossom said I had to wait. Now that you're here, enjoy."

Buttercup leaves without another word. Cerridwen's panicked eyes reach mine, and I mimic a deep breath. She follows along.

"Even if you are having your baby now, we will handle it," I reassure her. "But if your water hasn't broken, and Buttercup's tests confirm it's Braxton Hicks, that is likely the case. Have you had much water lately?"

Her guilty look tells her everything I need to know, and I give her soulmate a pointed look. Immediately, Zhu stops clutching her hand to retrieve Cerridwen some water, and her panic starts up again. I wasn't sure if her clinginess was part of having an alien baby, but Priscille didn't seem to need Mekho around thirty-three eight.

Since she's not breathing right, another uncomfortable pain squeezes her. It's reflected in her face. Then, she lets out the biggest gas bubble I've ever heard. Her face turns pink as she squeaks, "I feel a little better now."

I can't believe my mom's dying wish was for me to go to space. Do you think she knew in her last moments this is what it would look like? Fuck touching the stars. When I got back to Earth, I never wanted to see them again.

ACKNOWLEDGEMENTS

There are many people I would like to thank when it comes to Priscille's Alien Pirate, but here are my favorites this round.

Starting with the most important - thank you to all the readers who have picked up this series and stayed with me on the journey.

Next, thanks to my beta babes. Libby has stuck with me on this journey, with her willingness to provide detailed feedback and emphasize the parts of the book that were most enjoyable.

Finally, thank you to my local library and the group of writing friends I've found in my community. They heard alien pirates and space nuns, and they were all in. Support your local library!

BOOK CLUB DISCUSSION

1. Priscille and Mekho both change their path in life once they meet each other. Discuss the effects unexpected circumstances have had on your own life path.
2. Abbess Carlow plays a significant role in Priscille's life both by suggesting she join the sisters serving the SS Herculean and being a voice in her head. How do mentors and guidance figures influence the characters in the story?
3. Both Priscille and Mekho have experienced significant religious and existential crises. How do these crises shape their connection with each other and their search for meaning and purpose on Shojo?
4. How does Priscille's experience with domestic violence impact her ability to trust and open up to Mekho? How does their relationship evolve as she shares her trauma with him, and how does Mekho support her in her healing process?
5. This book is part of an ongoing series of interconnected standalones. What inferences can you make from Priscille's and Mekho's story about the upcoming books?

Thank you for reading "Priscille's Alien Pirate"! If you've enjoyed the book and would like to stay connected, here are some ways to do so:

Visit MadisonValePublishing.com

Sign up for our mailing list to receive exclusive content, book recommendations, and notifications about new releases directly in your inbox. Stay in the loop and be among the first to know about any exciting developments.

Follow @madi.vale on Instagram

Consider leaving a review of "Priscille's Alien Pirate" on platforms such as Goodreads, Amazon, or other book review websites.